HUNTER

MELISSA BELLE

Autumn Ink Press

ARE YOU A VIP?

Click here to join Melissa's VIP List and never miss a thing!

Sign up and get a free story! Plus stay up to date on hot sales, upcoming new releases, and exclusive content you can't get anywhere else.

ABOUT

Turns out we both need to score...a second chance, roommates-to-lovers hockey romance.

Hunter

I can't be alone. But I can't be in a relationship. And now I can't even score on the ice. I'm in a slump.

I figure an off-limits pet sitter is just what I need. Until I see who the agency sent me.

Winter Allen is standing all grown up at my front door.

She's my hat-trick: the looks, the heart, and the history.

I let her run off to Broadway because she deserved to follow her teenage dreams as much as I did.

We both got everything we wanted. So why does she look so damn lonely?

Winter

I didn't plan to see Hunter Storm again. And I don't plan to tell him why I'm back home in New Orleans.

But after one devilish grin, my body tells me Hunter's the only man who can help me.

Turns out we both need to score again. So who's to say it's a bad idea to mix his fire and my gasoline?

What are we doing? I'm not sure, but it feels too good to stop.

For Daddy, thanks for holding on tight to me—and your beer—while rooting for your favorite team. You were always a father before a fan, and I love you more than words can say.

CHAPTER ONE

Winter

From the backseat of the taxi, I stare out the dirty window at the city lights as the driver weaves his way through New Orleans.

He doesn't drive as crazy fast as the cab drivers in Manhattan, but my stomach's queasy anyway. Must be that fast food I picked up when I got off the plane nearly an hour ago.

I shake my head at myself. Who am I kidding?

My stomach's queasy because of where I'm headed.

Home.

The place I swore I'd never return—New Orleans, Louisiana —where all I ever talked about when I lived here was getting out. Even if I'm only here temporarily, it still feels too long. And coming home like this...I feel like a massive failure.

In just a few minutes, I'll pay the driver and step out into the heart of New Orleans—the French Quarter. I'll inhale the thick, humid air that reminds me so much of my childhood, air that always maintains a hint of the nearby Mississippi River. I can't deny I've missed the south, but the humidity does nothing good for my hair.

Beep-beep!

Slamming of brakes and we're at a red light. I glance out the window and my breath catches in my throat.

Cheer on the Fire with Hunter Storm!

My gaze snags on the digital billboard just ahead, and I can't tear my eyes away even as the light turns green. The taxi driver veers sharply, and I brace myself to avoid slamming my head against the window while I stare at the handsome dark-haired guy on the billboard. His cocky grin while he points with his index finger at the words "New Orleans' first professional ice hockey team welcomes you!" sends me into a near-meltdown of conflicting emotions.

I miss him.

I can't let him see me like this.

Fitting that I've been in town all of five minutes and Hunter Storm has already knocked me off-kilter. Just like he always did.

My phone rings and I answer it, grateful for the interruption.

"Hello, bestie."

"Yay, you answered! That must mean you've landed!" Peyton's cheery voice comes through the receiver clearly.

I swallow hard, wishing I felt a hundredth as happy as she does living here. Peyton Black has the perfect set-up—she and her boyfriend, Scott, travel the country for months at a time in their motorcoach, and they also spend time visiting his family in Europe. With her business and her parents and brother in New Orleans, Peyton has the wings and the roots, which is all I ever wanted.

"That's right. I've landed," I say, trying to sound positive.

"Oh, sugar, you're miserable already," she says in concern.

"I'm okay," I lie.

The driver winds through the streets of the French Quarter, and I glance around with interest. It may be nighttime, but the Quarter never sleeps, and people are bustling about the curved streets. The pet sitting job that I applied for is right near here, which was one of the things that drew me to the position. I grew up wishing I could walk around the city at leisure, and this will give me the chance.

In a couple of hours, I'll be meeting the pet owner at his place. But for now, I'm planning to grab a drink and relax by myself.

"How did your last audition go? The one for the lead on the new Broadway show?" Peyton interrupts my thoughts.

"Um..." I pause. "Not great. It was super competitive."

I don't tell her I bombed that audition, much like the one before, and that was the impetus for my manager insisting I take a few months' break and leave town.

"*Your voice is shot, Winter,*" Pat said. "*And you're not the same. Get out of the city for the spring and summer, and come back in the fall for audition season.*"

"*But I can't miss any time here,*" I protested. *We had just met for coffee around the corner from Times Square where Pat delivered the bad news about my latest failed audition.* "*I just got my big break. That's why I'm getting all these calls. You know that.*"

We both knew that one more blown audition might cement my reputation as a one-hit-wonder. But Pat was kind enough not to say anything. He just patted my shoulder and told me he'd stay in touch. And then he walked away, leaving me standing on the sidewalk with a half-empty cup of coffee and a nearly-finished career.

"I'm sorry, sugar. Let Scott and me take you out tonight," Peyton says, bringing me out of my thoughts. "We'll meet up with the others and go to the Riverway, not fancy like you and your big-star self are used to with all those Manhattan clubs, but it'll still be fun."

"That sounds great," I say. "But..." I hesitate and cut myself off.

Peyton's not one of my oldest friends for nothing. "Hunter won't be there," she promises. "Well, I can't swear that he won't be out and about, but everyone knows better than to invite him to come with us when you're going to be there."

"I appreciate that. I know our situation makes things awkward for the rest of you."

"We love you both. But you do know you're going to have to see him sometime," she says gently. "I mean, I know you're returning to New York, but you'll be here for a while, and the Storm brothers are hugely popular here. Especially once the ice hockey team came to town, and Liam and Hunt became its two biggest stars."

"I've already seen a billboard," I murmur as I signal to the driver to stop at the cafe on the right.

I pay my tab and step out as Peyton laughs.

"Yeah, well, Hunt's a big deal around here. You know that."

"It was easier when he played hockey elsewhere," I say as the driver retrieves my one suitcase from the back. "I could come home and know he wouldn't be around. But now that he's here..."

"I get it." Peyton's voice softens. "But he's definitely here now. And he's pretty much impossible to ignore. You'll see more than just the one billboard of the team around the city, and his handsome face is plastered on all of them."

"Have you gone out with him at all?" I never ask her about the boy from my past, but I'd rather know in advance than be surprised later.

"A few times," she says. "My brother's seen him a bunch. And not just at his games." She pauses. "Hunter's party side hasn't exactly let up since you left."

"I'm sure it hasn't. I know I'll have to deal with him eventually. I just need a little time to get my feet down first."

I don't want to admit to her that seeing Hunter Storm again is the hardest part about returning to New Orleans.

CHAPTER TWO

Hunter

I check the defender hard into the boards and win the battle for the puck.

Spinning around, I cradle the prize with my stick as I skate down the open ice toward the goal.

The goalie pushes out from the net to try to narrow down my angles, but I'm going too fast. With a quick flick of my wrist, I launch the puck off the end of my stick.

It zips past the goalie's outstretched glove but sails wide left and misses the net.

"Fuck," I growl as I race behind the goal.

I slam into the first defender before he reaches my errant shot, and Murph dislodges the puck from between him and the boards. Murph looks up and sees that Liam has a clear path to the net, and he sends the puck toward him. Liam fakes like he's going low with his shot, and at the last second, he flips the puck up past the goalie's stick and into the back of the net.

I breathe out in relief as the buzzer sounds.

"One to nothing," Liam says as he pounds me on the back. "We've still got a shot to win the division."

But when we skate over to the bench and file off the ice, Coach Jones isn't smiling.

"Nice going." Coach slaps Murph and Liam on the shoulders before turning to me. "You do what you need to do to get out of this funk, Storm. You hear me? Whatever it takes. You're our first-line left winger. I want to keep it that way."

His warning isn't subtle, and I know he meant it that way.

"Understood," I tell him. "I'm working through it."

"You need my help, just let me know."

"Yes, sir." I continue past him.

"Whatever it takes, Hunt," Liam says to me as he echoes our family motto. My brother's tone is determined like always. "Right?"

"Right."

Once we're off the ice and out of earshot of any media or coaches, Murph mutters to me, "We need you, Hunt. We got lucky tonight."

Dean, our best defenseman, catches up to us as we head for our lockers. "Fuck, yeah, we did." His blond hair is sweaty and sticking to his head as he removes his helmet and throws it into his locker. "We should have beat those guys going away."

I grimace. This slump has stretched for nearly four weeks. All of January, and now that we've hit February and nothing's changed, I'm starting to panic. But I don't say that.

Prior to January, I'd been having the best season of my career. There was talk of league MVP, and I was stoked. Lately, all that talk has cooled, and I just want to get back to what I know I'm capable of.

It was always my dream to play hockey for my home state of Louisiana—not to mention with my brothers. So when the New Orleans Fire got an expansion team three years ago, and my oldest brother, Liam, and I were picked up, it was a dream come true.

Our twin brothers, Jared and Max, were still under contract for the Montana Wild Kings, but New Orleans was able to snag Camden Murphy out of free agency. Murph is my childhood friend and brother in everything but his last name, and the three of us are feeling pretty damn lucky. We've got a great owner who's all in, and I want to pay him back for bringing me here by playing at an MVP level. But I can't do that unless I get myself out of this damn slump.

I open my locker and toss my helmet onto the shelf. I take off my skates and then start to strip off my jersey and shoulder pads.

"I know what the problem is," a familiar deep, gravelly voice says from my left. "You miss living with me, don't you, baby brother?"

I glance up. Wearing nothing but a towel around his waist, Liam leans against the locker next to mine. He's got his usual obnoxious grin on his ruggedly handsome face.

I cross my arms over my chest and set my jaw as I give my brother a hard look.

"Liam, back the fuck off. I don't need to live with you to get out of my slump."

"Kind of do, man." Murph nods seriously, his overgrown dark hair falling into his eyes.

"We've all got superstitions, right?" Dean says, his dark eyes serious. "Most athletes do. Yours is to have a roommate and make sure you stay the hell away from relationships."

Murph adds, "So how do you manage? Same way I do—you fuck on the regular. You're doing that part just fine. But the first one? Clearly, you need a new roommate." He turns to Liam. "You left him high and dry."

Liam shakes his head. "Wasn't meant that way. He swore he had a new housemate lined up. How was I to know he'd lied?"

"I didn't want you changing your plans for me," I say stubbornly. "I did have someone lined up. But he bailed at the last minute."

"Well, I've got a kid at home—and a wife," Liam says. "And

you, Dean, and Murph have got what? Another weekend picking up the flavor of the month?"

I look into my older brother's narrowed green eyes. Sometimes, it's like looking in the mirror. But I'd never tell him that.

"You were just like us until Cathy got pregnant and you two decided to make a go of it," I say, giving it right back to him.

Liam's jaw turns to stone, and he runs his hand through the same dark wavy hair we can both thank our late father for.

"Watch it, little brother," he growls.

I tug at my own hair that's plastered to my head from sweat. "I'm happy for you; don't misunderstand me." I raise my hands in a surrender gesture. "I'm just saying—don't judge me because a part of you still wants to be free and easy."

And...I've touched a nerve.

"I love my kid, okay?" Liam's face is suddenly inches from mine. "And I love my wife. Just because the only girl you ever loved left town..."

I push him into the lockers. He may be older than me, but I've got three inches and twenty pounds on him. Being the tallest in the family comes in handy when you're the youngest of four boys.

"Jesus, Hunt," Liam says as I hold him hostage. "I'm sorry, okay? Winter just pushes all your buttons. She always did."

I press Liam harder against the lockers and pin his arm behind his back. "You better quit talking, big brother."

As usual, he doesn't listen. "Why don't you move on and find a nice girl to settle down with?" he says. "Then you'd have a permanent roommate and wouldn't be screwing up our playoff hopes."

At his last words, I still. "You're clearly not listening. I don't do relationships." Relationships are inherently messy, and I need to put all my focus on my career.

"Hey!" Coach Jones steps into our space and separates me from Liam. "Ease up, Storms. There's media around. You two brothers want to go somewhere private so you can beat the shit out of each other like you're kids again? No problem. But not here. Not when you're with the team."

Coach Jones may not have played in the pros, but he was a star college player, and he's still in excellent shape. He has no problem shoving Liam and me apart, nor any hesitation in giving us both a lethal staredown.

I back off, apologize to Coach, and grab my towel. I peel off the rest of my padding and uniform, wrap the towel around my waist, and head for the showers.

Murph and Dean catch up to me.

"Let's get drinks after this," Murph suggests. "Blow off some steam."

"Can't," I say. "I've got to remedy my living situation, remember?"

"You have a plan?" He raises one dark, bushy eyebrow in surprise.

"Sure I do. I have a pet sitter moving in to care for my cat. I'm gone so much I was paying through the nose for last-minute care by strangers I don't trust to do a good job, and I hate leaving her at a kennel. So, this will take care of two of my problems. Plus, I've got a late night planned with Deb."

"So, you'll get yourself a housemate in the form of a pet sitter, which also resolves your cat care problem." Murph holds up a finger. "And you've got plans with your on and off fuck buddy." He holds up a second finger. "Those two things should kill the slump, right?"

"Right." They better, or I could lose my place on the first line. And worse, we could miss the playoffs altogether. I've worked too damn hard for that to happen.

"Who's the pet sitter?" Dean asks.

I shrug. "Someone who knows the French Quarter. She used to live in New Orleans years ago. I asked for an older lady who won't be impressed by my profession, preferably someone who doesn't follow hockey at all. The agent told me she had it handled, and she's making sure the woman signs an NDA."

"Huh. A chick. Well, as long as you don't fuck her, right?" Dean says. "That will just complicate things."

"I'm not interested in screwing around with a live-in. You guys know that."

Murph shoots me a warning look. "And I know you, Hunt. Just remember, a roommate, even if she's hot, is off-limits."

***

Winter

I enjoy my time at the cafe before grabbing another cab and giving him the address of my temporary home.

It's a short drive, and I exhale as the cab comes to a stop outside a stand-alone residence. I pay the driver and grab my one suitcase. The rest of my stuff will be delivered to my parents' house tomorrow, so I'm traveling light. At least I don't have to live with my parents. I'll see them plenty, but the idea of moving back into my childhood bedroom is a bit too much.

I look up at the house before me curiously.

It's freshly painted in white with blue trim. It's much better taken care of than I'd expected it to be. I had assumed the place would have a barely lived-in feel, because the agent I spoke with explained how the owners are rarely home, but that they don't like to move their cat every time they leave on business. She said the owners are a young couple with a baby and that the man's line of work is rather "unconventional," but she didn't elaborate. And I didn't ask. This is New Orleans—unconventional could mean literally anything.

It's a two-story, townhouse-style home with a cute front porch and upper balcony. Being in the city, it's right next to the neighboring homes, but it has a driveway that leads into the back of the lot, and the entire property has a warm, homey feeling. And the location can't be beat. It's on a quiet side street only a block from Jackson Square.

The agent from the pet sitting service told me the owners would be home to meet me and show me around the place, so I climb the front steps. Catching sight of the sign that reads

Come inside porch to find doorbell, I push through the screen door and step inside the porch, and that's when I come face to furry face with a handsome, orange-striped cat sitting on a porch swing and looking up at me with interest. I go to give it a quick pat.

"You're a sweetheart," I murmur into the kitty's long fur. "I could definitely take care of you."

The enclosed screen makes more sense now—it's a perfect space for a cat to hang out.

Before I can press the doorbell, I hear the door to the house open, and I straighten up. The wooden door opens outward, and it stands between me and the owner of the house, so I take the few steps around.

And...I suck back my gasp at who's standing in the doorway. *Holy. Shit.*

For the first time in ten years, I stare up into the deep green eyes of Hunter Storm.

I immediately start shaking. I don't know if he notices. He seems a little preoccupied staring at my breasts.

He's so...masculine. His eyes are greener than I remembered. His dark, wavy hair's a little more tamed except for one lock that still falls over his forehead. His jaw is set and strong.

And Jesus, he's built. I get that he's a professional athlete, but wow...he's grown up nice. He's all man now.

I watch the muscles in Hunter's forearm flex as he braces his arm against the door. The urging to touch him is too strong, too scary. But God, how I want to.

I picked up the phone to call him a thousand times over the last ten years—

When I blew my first audition and was sitting on the steps of my dorm room at NYU, crying my eyes out;

When I broke up with three guys in a week because none of them made me feel a millionth of what I felt when I was with him;

When I found out backstage I had to replace the lead of

Seasonal Bliss and was certain I was going to throw up from terror.

And of course, the last time I almost called him was when my world was falling apart.

I always dialed his number but then hung up before he answered. And now, he's standing right in front of me.

Holy. Shit.

CHAPTER THREE

Hunter

I open the door to let Theo inside.

Then someone steps around the corner into the doorway.

I suck in a breath as my world tips on its axis like it hasn't done in ten years.

Winter Princess Allen.

Her mouth drops open, and we stare at each other in silence.

"You're supposed to be my new boss," she finally says, immediately reaching for the spaghetti straps of her tank top, straps that have fallen off her shoulders, exposing creamy skin underneath.

I don't speak or move at first. I just take her in for a long minute—

Same chest-length black hair that I used to bury my fingers in;

Bewitching red pout that could swear like a sailor;

And almond-shaped blue eyes that saw right through me like nobody else ever could.

Her pink frilly skirt is short enough that I can see the scar on her mid-thigh she got when she slipped in the lake and cut herself on a rock. The thin fabric of her top hides absolutely nothing, and her nipples are poking against the fabric, practically daring me to touch them. Her feet are in open-toed sandals, as usual, and her toenails are painted pink. Cotton candy pink, I think she used to correct me.

Winter looks as startled to see me as I am her.

"How'd you know where I live?" I say in a far-more accusatory tone than I mean.

She furrows her eyebrows. "I don't know where you live. I'm here for the couple needing a pet sitter. *Shit*. Did I get the address wrong?"

She starts flipping through her phone.

Crap. I reach out and catch her wrist. "Don't bother. This is the right place."

Her eyes widen.

"You're the couple with the cat? The agency said the man travels a lot."

I gesture to the New Orleans Fire sweatshirt I'm wearing. "Road trip next week."

She sighs. "Oh Lord."

Oh Lord is right. I raise an eyebrow at her. "So you want a tour of the place?"

She looks at me like I'm nuts. "Right. Like you and I could live together peaceably. No, I'll just be on my way. My parents will be thrilled to see me, anyway. You know my father—always convinced the square is filled with murderers."

But after seeing Winter again for the first time in years, I'm not about to let her go that easily.

"You already came all this way." I step out onto the porch, and she inhales. "Do you want to come in? Or are you afraid you won't be able to control yourself if you get too close to me?"

She covers with a forced smile. "Did you know I was coming home?"

My short laugh cuts through the bullshit, and she blushes. No man could make Winter blush but me. No one else could get through that layer of superiority her mother trained her in so well.

"Yeah, and I made sure to hire you. Because we ended things so well the last time." I try to say it jokingly, but the pain between us lingers.

One thing Winter and I always know how to do is fight. Ever since we were kids, we would get each other going. When we were young, those fights ended in making up with ice cream cones by the lake, and when we got older...let's just say a good fight between Winter and me finished in an even hotter make-out session.

She bites her lip like she knows what I'm thinking.

I watch her gather herself, put on her polite face, and nod. "Pardon my manners. I left Manhattan before dawn, so I didn't get a proper night's sleep."

But I can't let go of the thought nagging at me. "So why are you home, Winter? I figured a big Broadway star like you would be too busy these days to visit Louisiana. You just decided to come home for a while?"

She hesitates, and I can tell she's debating whether to tell a white lie or go for the truth.

When she exhales heavily and purses her lips, I know she's about to tell me the truth cloaked in some kind of a white lie.

"I hurt my vocal cords performing," she says in a voice so sad I nearly reach for her. "My manager sent me home. So, no more Broadway auditions until the fall."

I'm not sure which of the above was a lie, or maybe she simply omitted something. Either way, she didn't give me the whole story. But I'm not about to call her out on it right now. She's clearly in some kind of pain, and the last thing she needs is me being a dick.

"I'm sorry," I say gruffly.

"Thank you."

Ten seconds of us assessing each other in silence.

Yep. The chemistry's still there. Winter Allen can still rev me up like no other woman. And she's still off-limits—she was never meant to stay with me. She had her Broadway dreams to pursue, and hell if I was going to be the asshole to hold her back.

And I had my own dreams. Since we were kids, my three brothers and I were laser-focused on ice hockey. Sounds absolutely nuts to have a hockey dream in a southern city that, honest to God, didn't always have an ice hockey rink, but we caught hockey fever from watching the college and pro games on TV with our dad. He made sure we could go to camps every summer, and we travelled to Baton Rouge to play in a local club league that's since defunct.

Somehow, all four of us made the pros.

But my other dream—the one that involved Winter—apparently wasn't meant to be.

It's not like she and I ever even dated. We were...undefined. We weren't quite friends, and we weren't quite lovers—we were everything and nothing to each other, all at once.

So, I supported her Broadway dreams, and she supported my hockey ones. She'd leave town frequently to study in Manhattan, and I'd be gone in the summers for weeks at a time, practicing hockey. Somehow, our dual obsessive natures matched up. Our chemistry was nuclear, and no one could get my attention like she could.

But we were too singularly focused on our goals to have room for a real relationship. And when Winter moved to New York right after high school graduation as planned, to attend college and major in performing arts with her eye on Broadway, I stuck with my plan to attend college locally and throw all my energy into getting drafted.

She and I drifted apart like people do when they don't see each other for years. To get through it, I put up a wall and firmly shut the door on keeping in touch.

But I was young and stubborn then. Now I'm older and slightly less obstinate.

"I've kept tabs on you, you know."

Winter's lips part. "You have?"

I can't believe I just revealed my hand, but no sense in holding back now. "I have." I look her right in the eyes when I say, "I'm fucking proud of you, Princess. You've done good."

The polite expression on her face eases, and she says, "Thank you, Hunt. That means a lot. And just so you know—I watch as many of your games as I can on TV. No matter whether you've been in Phoenix or New Orleans, I cheer for your team."

This surprises me. Winter always supported me unconditionally, but we ended in a fight...probably the only way we could say goodbye without it killing either of us.

"You cheered for the Phoenix Hawks?" I tease her.

"I cheered for *you*, Hunt. Wherever you were playing. I'm so proud of you, too."

"Thanks." I clear my throat, desperate to get rid of the emotion suddenly clogging it. "So you applied for this pet sitting job to avoid living at the Allen Jail?"

She breaks form at my joke, and a beautiful smile fills her face. That one dimple on her left cheek was always my undoing.

"Pretty much. But the rest of my time in New Orleans?" She holds up her hands. "Still figuring it out."

Something doesn't add up.

"What about your lead role in Seasonal Bliss? That must have opened a lot of doors, huh?"

She shifts from one foot to the other and looks past me out the window.

"Um...I've had issues auditioning. I've screwed up my last few."

I'm stumped. How could Winter be blowing her big break? She always relished the pressure; the bigger the spotlight, the brighter she shined.

But she clearly doesn't want to talk about it.

"Well, pet sitting is a fun gig too. Could teach you a few things in case you ever have to act alongside a cat."

Her smile doesn't reach her eyes. "Right."

I inhale.

I could stand here and talk to Winter forever. She's mesmerizing and fascinating and as complex and beautiful as she always was. But I can't look for something in a woman who's only here for six months max.

I open the door wide. "Come on. I'll show you around the house. No one knows better than I do the torture you're gonna be in for if you live with your parents while you're here."

Her mouth opens and then closes. I can practically see the wheels churning in her mind.

"The city's crowded, Winter. And not everyone who advertises for a pet sitter should be trusted."

She inhales so sharply I hear it catch in her throat.

"You okay?" I ask her.

"Yes," she stammers. "Fine. But I don't think you and I are good housemates material."

"Maybe not, but the chances of finding a safe place for rent this short notice is nil. Plus, you get a twofer—me and Theo here." I gesture to the cat, who's watching us both closely.

"What about your..." She almost seems to force the next word out. "Wife? Or is it girlfriend? And your..." Another pause before she says in nearly a whisper, "Baby?"

CHAPTER FOUR

I cock my head. "I'm not following. It's just me here, Win. That's why I need someone to look after Theo when I'm away."

She exhales. "The agency told me you had a family—and I *know* she mentioned a baby."

I hold up my hands. "I ain't got no baby, darling. Don't you think Peyton or Ash would have mentioned that to you?"

She shakes her head. "Outside of hockey, I ask my friends not to relay any personal information about you."

Ouch. "Well, I'm not a daddy. The agency must have gotten their information mixed up. I told them my brother moved out of here because he had a baby and got married. In that order."

Her eyes soften. "Which brother?"

"Liam. Max and Jared are still playing hockey for the Montana Wild Kings."

"That's right. Well, congratulations to Liam." Winter reaches over to pet Theo. "So he and Cathy stayed together, huh?"

"Yeah. When Cathy got pregnant, and then she gave birth and they tied the knot, this place just felt too small for them. Didn't want his little brother hanging around anymore while he changed diapers, I guess."

"Did you change any diapers?"

"Of course. I changed plenty of Lulu's diapers. She's my goddaughter and my favorite person in the world."

Winter's pretty pink lips part. "That's sweet, Hunt."

I touch Winter's sandaled foot with my bare one. "So you'll move in and take care of Theo here? You get your own suite."

She stares up at me. "Won't this kind of...suck? You and I haven't exactly been close lately. I can explain to the agency that I'm the one who turned the job down, and I'm sure they can find you someone else who's qualified."

I swallow hard. "I want you, Winter." *Always have.*

Our eyes lock. Whether or not she sees what's surely written all over my face—that nothing's changed since we were kids—I don't know.

Until she says gently, "You still can't live alone, Hunt?"

I look past her at Theo. "I've got Theo."

"You thought he'd be enough to kill the memories?" she asks in a strangled tone like she's reliving my father's murder as much as I am.

I force myself to meet her gaze. "I don't know. Maybe?"

She nods. "I get it. Okay. I'll give it a try."

I take Winter's hand in mine and lead her into the house.

"Will sure suck for me," I joke, "to have to see your Princess face every morning across the breakfast table."

She laughs.

Her hand still fits in mine. I should let it go, but I don't. Instead, I hold onto her all the way down the hallway and into the living room.

And she doesn't pull away.

We break apart awkwardly when she spins around to look at my place.

"The balcony must have a great view."

"You can use it whenever you like," I say.

"I can't believe this is yours." She holds my gaze. "Good for you."

"Thanks." My voice comes out gruff.

I show her through the rest of the house, trying not to sound like an ass when I point out the bathroom and kitchen I remodeled after Liam and I bought the place.

"This is amazing, Hunt." She stops in the middle of the kitchen. "It feels so warm."

I swallow, and the frustration of how well she fits in my house bubbles up in my throat and threatens to come out.

Instead, I turn on my heel and lead her up the short flight of stairs. "And here's the guest suite. You've got your own bathroom."

She exclaims over the soaking tub and then wanders into the bedroom. She takes in the king-sized bed against the back wall and flanked by two windows. The walls are a pale green, and the only flaw in the space is a large dent in the door.

Winter looks right at it.

I start stammering something about Liam and his stupid temper, but she cuts me off with a smile.

"Let me guess—you two went at it one night after a few beers, and somebody missed a punch?"

The heat prickles the back of my neck and threatens to rise up into my face. "I'd never miss on a punch—you think I'd give up a chance to hit my brother?"

She throws back her head and laughs.

And I relax. I lean back against the door jam and smile at her. Those blue eyes of hers fix on mine like lasers until—

"So how did Cathy enjoy living here?" she asks, breaking the silence. "Can a woman handle this place, or will I run screaming back to my parents' house after the first night?"

"Darling, no woman runs screaming from me," I say slowly. "Although, you've always been the exception to that rule, haven't you?"

Her face flushes red, and she steps closer to me. She grabs two of the belt loops on my jeans and pulls me flush to her.

"I never ran from you, Hunter." Her breath is hot and smells like lemons.

"Pretty sure we both ran," I mutter as my hands go around her back and slide underneath her top.

I nearly lose my shit when my fingers land on the hot, soft, smooth skin of her back. The heat between her legs hits my sudden erection, and I swallow a groan. I rub my thumbs in circles over the small of her back, and she presses into me further.

"Are you seeing someone?" she asks in nearly a whisper. "Is there a woman I should know about who'll be staying here every night?"

Her blue eyes are flecked with violet, but the purple shade darkens to black as we stare at each other.

"No woman," I say in a rough voice. "You know I'm not into commitment."

I slowly drag one of my hands around her side. When I reach her stomach, she jumps backward so fast she bangs her head against the nearby lamp.

I widen my eyes. "What's wrong?"

She averts her gaze and reaches into her purse. When she produces her phone, I know she's intent on getting out of here before we finish this conversation. Well, that's not going to happen.

"Winter." I follow her out into the hallway. "Hey."

She calls for a cab before catching her lower lip between her teeth. I get a glimpse of the haunted look in her eyes before she ducks her head and charges for the front door.

"So I'll bring my stuff by tomorrow morning, okay?" she says over her shoulder. "I'll leave my suitcase here."

"Hey. Spoiled Southern Princess. Talk to me." I'm desperate to get her to slow down, and I use the name that pisses Winter off more than any other.

But even that doesn't get a rise out of her. She just gives me the smallest of smiles before darting out the door and down the walkway.

I step out onto the front porch. Within thirty seconds, I

hear the squeal of tires, and I watch as the taxi she's jumped into disappears.

I stare down the empty street and shake my head.

Something just fucking happened. I didn't imagine it.

I run my hand over my face as I look down at Theo.

He looks back at me like he knows exactly what's going on and I'm the only idiot standing here in the dark.

I frown at him. "How the fuck do you know? You just met her. I've known her my whole damn life!"

Another haughty glance hits me before Theo starts cleaning his paws.

"Fine," I say to him. "So you're smarter than I am. But you're also a cat. So you have some limitations with women. I'm going to use all the tools at my disposal to figure out exactly what Winter Princess Allen's secrets are. I've got nothing better to do."

I've never had anything better to do than figure out Winter. And now that I'm going to be living with her in the same house, I can do just that.

I reach for my phone to cancel my date with Deb. As much as meeting up with her would no doubt help my tension, I'm no longer in the mood to see any woman but one.

CHAPTER FIVE

Winter

I stare out the window as the taxicab hurtles me through the French Quarter.

I wanted to kiss Hunter so badly, more than I've wanted anything in a very long time.

But the pain of what happened six months ago stopped me cold. Just like it's been stopping me from nailing an audition.

My hormones are firing on all cylinders, and I swear my nipples are still hard from Hunter's eyes on them. If I'd known ahead of time that I'd be living with him, I would have used my vibrator as much as possible in Manhattan to get any feelings of need out of my system. Because not having been with someone in ages, combined with my combustible reaction whenever I'm within a hundred feet of Hunter Storm, has me all sorts of crazy right now.

The lighted sign for Shoes Galore pops into view, and I call out for the driver to stop.

I need to see my parents, but I'm going to take a detour and visit my best friend first.

I pay the cab fare and hop out. The store sign says closed, but I can see Peyton through the glass. She stands on her toes to fix a set of sandals on, and I smile. Her dark hair shines in the lights, and as usual, she's rocking an absolutely perfect pair of shoes.

I knock on the glass door lightly. Peyton turns around and immediately runs to the door and opens it for me.

Then, she pulls me into a huge hug.

"Look at you!" She holds out her arms. "You look amazing! I love your shoes!"

"You gave them to me!" I say with a laugh. "And I noticed yours from outside." I gesture to her red heels. "They're awesome."

"While you look amazing..." She studies my face. "You seem upset, Win. Is everything all right?"

I wish I could tell her the truth. Because I have no doubt she'd understand.

But, right now, I need help with...

"Hunter Storm is my boss."

Peyton's eyes go wide. "What—"

"And my new housemate. All in one."

"Holy shit."

"I know."

She reaches behind her cash register, grabs her purse, and slips her arm through mine. "This kind of problem requires alcohol to sort out. Let's go to The Riverway."

———

"Wow," I say as Peyton leads me up the stairs inside The Riverway and over to a free set of couches positioned around a gas fireplace. "This place is gorgeous."

Music drifts up from Jackson Square, and Peyton and I settle across from each other on a couch.

"Blaire owns this place, right?" I ask Peyton.

Blaire is Peyton's sister-in-law. She's married to Peyton's

brother, Oliver, another classmate from my childhood that I grew up with.

Peyton slips off her shoes and tucks her feet underneath her on the couch. "She does. I can't believe you've never been here."

"I haven't been back since Blaire returned to New Orleans," I remind her. "I only met her the one time you all came to see me in New York."

"I know. I just always remember you here." She laughs. "I sound like a grandmother or something."

I understand what she means. Time seems to stop when you're at home.

Blaire approaches us with a smile. She's a tall redhead with a killer style. Today, she's wearing a flared black skirt and classy silk top. She's totally Oliver's type, and I love that they found each other.

I don't know her well, but Blaire surprises me with a warm hug. "Welcome home," she says to me.

"Thank you."

She studies my face. "If you're feeling anything close to what I was when I returned home, you may not be as excited as we all are that you're here."

I laugh. "It's been an adjustment, that's for sure."

"Take your time adjusting," she advises me. "It's different for everyone."

"Winter's got a boy problem already," Peyton says to her.

Blaire sits down on the adjacent couch. "Tell me. I'm a bartender. I can help."

I throw up my hands. "I don't think anyone can help me with Hunter Storm."

Blaire's eyes widen. "Hunter Storm, the star of the New Orleans Fire? I've met him through Oliver. They don't hang out a lot, but you all grew up together, right?"

"We did," I say. "He and I were pretty close."

Peyton snorts. "That's an understatement. Those two were so into each other. I still can't believe you never dated."

Me neither. "Timing," I say in a forced tone. "We were both so career-oriented."

"He's hot as hell," Blaire says with a teasing smile in my direction.

"He is," I agree. "That's a fact. But he's...complicated."

"He seems like he'd be pretty intense," Blaire says.

"He's had to deal with some difficult stuff." Peyton's voice turns sad. "Hunter's daddy was murdered when the boys were teenagers. The police never found the murderer."

Blaire sighs. "How tragic. Aren't all four Storm brothers in the pros?"

I nod. "They were single-minded in that. Their dad was their biggest fan. Once he was gone, I think they all felt like they owed it to him to make it."

"Well, it's incredible that they all did." Blaire looks at me. "So what's the backstory between you and Hunter?"

"They had endless 'almosts' but never sealed the deal," Peyton says before I can speak.

I gesture toward Peyton. "What she said. And I can't live with him now," I add, hating how vulnerable I sound when I say it. "The risk feels ridiculously large. I was there for all of ten minutes, and I already had trouble keeping my hands off of him."

"Win and Hunter have a nuclear attraction," Peyton says to Blaire. "It's even hot to watch them flirt. You'll see."

"You *won't* see," I say. "Because I can't socialize with him." I turn to Peyton. "Maybe you can set me up with somebody harmless and safe while I'm here, someone I can flirt with but not actually desire. Someone who doesn't come with a giant warning label like Hunter Storm."

Peyton and Blaire burst out laughing. "That sounds like the opposite of boyfriend material," Blaire says. "Or even hot fling material. Why would you want to date someone you don't even want?"

I play it off with a laugh, but inside, I'm shaking. The idea of being with any man after being attacked by one...it just doesn't feel possible right now. Maybe someday, but not yet.

"So, what are you going to do about your living situation?" Peyton asks me.

I shake my head. "I have no fucking clue."

I came home to heal, and Hunter and I...we're too combustible to be healthy.

Besides, the darkness that's surrounded me for the past six months has been threatening to engulf me utterly, and I haven't found the exit door to escape my pain.

What happened to me could have happened to anyone.

I tell myself that every day. But the shame and the fear eat away at me anyway. Being attacked put me in a place of vulnerability where now, every time I step outside, I feel exposed. Like the world knows my secret and there's not a damn thing I can do about it. Every morning, I get up and look out at the sun, praying today will be the day the world will stop feeling black.

Seeing Hunter again is the first time I felt a ray of sunshine return to my soul.

The easy banter we still had with each other and the way he looked at me, I felt...wanted. Desired. But I know him—he won't be satisfied with surface-level chit-chat. He never was. So I need to keep him at arm's length. Because I don't want anyone to know why Pat really sent me home, and if I let him in, Hunter won't give up until he learns the truth.

CHAPTER SIX

Hunter

I show up at the Allen mansion early the next morning. I figure Winter could use some help moving her stuff, and I don't have practice until later. Wanting to see her again to make sure she doesn't change her mind on moving in with me has nothing to do with it. *Right.*

The Allens live on the other side of the city from where I grew up. The rich side of the Big Easy. I may be living well now, but it wasn't always that way. My mama died when we were all young, and my dad did his best to make ends meet. He ran a convenience store that doubled as a gas station, and we spent hours there after school. It seemed like a good gig for him. Until he was shot and killed one night in a robbery hold-up.

I step out of my truck and try to ignore the lurching feeling in the pit of my stomach. I haven't been here in years, and the last time I left, I swore it would be the last.

I take off my baseball cap and head up the perfectly-manicured walkway toward the house. The chirping birds and bright sky belie my sense of foreboding as I get closer and closer to the front door Mr. Allen threw me out of on more than one occasion for being a "bad influence on his daughter."

I reach the red wooden door and ring the bell. The doorbell sounds the same: large and brass and irritating.

A long wait before the door finally swings open, and Mrs. Allen greets me.

"Hello, Hunter." She frowns, not bothering to hide her dislike of me. Becoming a hockey star didn't change her opinion of me—that I come from the wrong side of the tracks and was never good enough for her daughter.

They gave Winter the middle name "Princess" for a reason—they want her to go through life not wanting for anything, and they expect that her husband will be able to give her the world. Even though I could do that now, the Allens will never see me that way. And in truth, I don't know that I see myself that way either. I never forgot where I came from.

"Ma'am." I nod politely. "I'm here to help Winter move her things."

"Come on inside." She takes a second look at me, and I know she's about to ask me for a favor. Winter's parents have never been shy about taking what they want. "I seem to remember you being handy around the house. Must be that blue-collar upbring-ing." She sniffs.

I barely resist a laugh. "Must be. What do you need help with, Mrs. Allen?"

She beckons me toward the stairs. "Come with me."

———

Winter

The buzzing sound of a weed whacker wakes me early in the morning.

I didn't miss that when I lived in Manhattan. For some reason, the sounds of traffic and sirens disturbed me less. And my parents always make sure their lawn is perfectly manicured, which means an excessive amount of lawn care.

I had a fitful night of sleep, and as I become fully awake, I expect to be greeted by that familiar foreboding feeling I've had for the past six months. Instead, Hunter pops into my head. The memory of him touching me yesterday is so strong that I actually miss him.

The thing is—I don't just miss him. I *crave* him. I want him so much suddenly that my hand is beneath my underwear in seconds. I stifle a moan as my fingers fly across my clit. All I'm thinking about is Hunter and an image of him looking at me with that unmistakable hunger in his eyes. We never had sex, but we did other things, and those things were always...hot.

My face is heated and my breaths coming in short gasps when I hear—

"Hunter, right this way."

What is he doing here?

The footsteps are growing closer, and they stop just outside my bedroom door when Mama says, "I need you to change the faucets out in Winter's bathroom. If she's not awake yet, she should be. Let me just..."

I'm up out of the bed in a flash. Certain my cheeks are bright red and everything about me screams, "I've been touching myself," I dive headfirst into my massive walk-in closet, closing the door behind me.

My mother's knocks on the bedroom door are loud and firm. "Winter? Are you decent? Hunter's going to fix those dreadful faucets out and fix the god-awful leak!"

Hoping I can sneak out once Hunter's immersed himself in his task, I stay quiet.

Mama enters first. "Oh, she must have gotten up and I missed her downstairs somehow. Well, that's easy enough to do in our spacious home. Okay, Hunter, come with me into the bathroom here."

Shit. I left my bra hanging on the towel rack.

I listen at the closet door, but their voices are too low for me to make out any words. The majority of my clothing from New

York is in suitcases downstairs, but I'm not going to risk seeing Hunter again in these see-through pajamas.

I reach into a box I shipped from New York a year ago and grab the first clothing options I can find—which ends up being tiny jean cut-offs I haven't worn in years; a hot pink bikini top because my only available bra is currently in the bathroom with Hunter; and a gray NYU sweatshirt from a guy my castmate set me up with. I don't even know why I shipped the sweatshirt. The guy and I went out one time, and I basically shut the door on him when all he wanted to do was kiss me good night.

I throw on the cut-offs, top, and sweatshirt, still so wet from my Hunter fantasy a few minutes ago that the jeans press against me uncomfortably when I move. Not to mention I'm fully sexually frustrated in this moment, and the object of my morning desire is about five feet away. But he's with my mother, of course, just to ruin the fantasy.

I hear my mother leave the room, and I consider waiting it out until Hunter's done, but that could be a while. And I need to pee.

I open the closet door quietly and slip out. I tiptoe across my floor.

Maybe Hunter will be too busy fixing the sink to notice me.

"Morning, Princess."

No such luck.

I turn toward the open bathroom door and lock eyes with him.

"Morning."

He's looking fine. He smiles at me, and my gaze travels down his face and keeps going. And...

Sweet Lord.

My toes curl.

Hunter is shirtless, his t-shirt sitting uselessly on the sink counter behind him. His worn jeans ride low on his hips. All those muscles he uses to play professional ice hockey are on full display.

I don't even try to hide my staring.

His abs are literally an eight-pack, and his chest is defined and lightly dusted with dark hair. No fat anywhere I can see.

I haven't seen Hunter without a shirt on since high school. He was always built, but he was a teenager then. Now, he's all man, and I actually feel my stomach clench with need.

Forcing myself to look away, I point at the sink. "How did you get roped into helping with this?"

"Your mama asked. Like she always does. You know."

Right. My mother doesn't ask at all. She just demands.

"I'm sorry about that," I say. "But what were you doing here in the first place?"

"I wanted to help you move. I've got a truck. Figured we could put your things in the back."

"That's so thoughtful, Hunt." I smile at him. "My mama's lending me her spare car to use while I'm living here, so I can follow you back."

"Sounds good. I've got an extra parking space in the driveway. Let me just finish up here first."

He squats down and slides underneath the sink. I glance over toward the window.

Shit. My bra is still hanging on the rack. I walk over and grab it, shoving it behind the stacked towel set that's sitting behind the toilet.

"Can you hand me a wrench?" he asks.

I find it in his toolbox and hand it to him. And, even though I should probably leave and let him work, I don't want to. So I take a seat on the edge of the tub and admire his flexing abs as he fiddles with the plumbing.

"Where did you come from just now?" he asks me. "Your mama and I walked right through your room, and no one was in there."

"I was dressing in the closet," I say.

Hunter accepts my explanation, and we lapse into silence for the next ten minutes.

"All set." He slides out from underneath the sink and stands up.

His arm muscles flex as he pulls on a blue t-shirt, his same favorite color he's had since high school.

I stand, too, and his eyes catch mine. I fidget under the heat of his stare.

He looks down at my sweatshirt and then back up to my face.

"What the hell are you wearing?"

"What's it look like? Cut-offs, a hot pink bikini top, which I'm sure you noticed..."

He lifts an eyebrow. "Your sweatshirt is see-through."

"It's not see-through. It's a pale gray, so the pink shines through the...oh, never mind. It's just some guy's sweatshirt." I shrug. "My clothes got packed in a hurry, and I don't have my shit organized yet."

"Who's some guy?" he asks me.

His bright green eyes flash.

My face heats, and I tap my bare foot against the bathroom tile. "Nobody."

Hunter shrugs, and we look at each other in silence. Just as it's starting to feel like a stand-off, he reaches out and touches my hip.

I swallow.

He drops his hand, and I step back. But I can smell the familiar scent of his aftershave, and my chest aches for what we had. For what we could have had if we hadn't both been racing toward our dreams like the world would explode if we didn't get there.

And we both got exactly what we wanted. I hope to hell his dream made him happier than mine made me.

Hunter's eyes are on me like he's wondering what I'm thinking about. When I keep the eye contact, he gives me one of his rare grins.

The kind that always made me melt.

The kind I used to think about when I was alone in my bedroom with the shades drawn and could barely stand the stress and the loneliness of the self-imposed pressure I felt to be a star.

Hunter was the only person in my life who never bought into the persona of Winter Princess Allen. My friends didn't mean to, but they thought my dream to be a big Broadway star made me happy. Hunter used to say that he was just as proud of me for living as he was for anything I actually did.

I wonder if he still feels that way, or if whatever tied us together has become too frayed at this point. When I left for New York, we swore we'd stay friends. But like lots of things, that didn't go as we planned. He got drafted, we both got busy, and life marched on. In the blink of an eye, ten years had passed. But here we are, and I've got six months to get to know him all over again.

"What are you thinking about, Win?"

His deep voice drags me out of my thoughts.

I'm feeling flirty, which is a dangerous thing when I'm around Hunter. But I don't care right now.

I cock my head at him and smile.

"What are *you* thinking about, Mr. Storm? Something in particular?"

He's still grinning. "Sure."

I put one hand on my hip. "Well? What is it?"

"Will you take off some guy's sweatshirt if I ask you to?"

I kick him in the shin and he laughs.

"Like you've never seen me in a bikini before."

"Not in a long time."

His eyes darken with heat, and I sway closer to him.

His hand goes back to my hip. "It's good to see you, Winter. You look all grown up."

"So do you." My hand's now on his chest.

"Hunter!!"

My mother's shriek echoes up from the first floor.

I pull away, and he drops his hand at the same time.

"You're such a flirt." He's teasing me, but his voice has changed back to guarded.

I purse my lips and resist the burning urge I have to knee him in the balls. "You're such a guy. Why can't you just admit you were the one who started it?"

"I admit I was flirting." His gaze narrows. "But you won't admit to anything you're feeling. You never did. Not unless..."

He cuts off, but I know what he was about to say. Not unless I was naked and turned on...that's the only time I said what was in my heart.

"Oh, so you're saying I'm a coward?" I lift my chin and dare him to keep going.

"Hunter!!" Mama's voice is getting closer.

But we don't stop. Like it's always been between Hunter and me, we go from casual banter to full-on fighting in an instant.

"Not exactly." Hunter's jaw ticks. "But just because you can star on Broadway doesn't make you brave."

"Well, just because you can handle a hockey stick better than anyone in New Orleans doesn't make you happy," I counter just as my mother enters the bathroom.

"Honestly, Winter," Mama says. "Watch your tongue, young lady."

"Mama, don't say anything," I say as I turn toward her.

But that's like asking for the impossible.

"Don't speak that way to the help. You have better manners than that."

Mama's well-pressed navy suit is conservative and impeccable, and her dyed, black, bobbed hair is groomed to perfection. But her eyes are hard as they focus on me.

My cheeks flush with humiliation, and I can't even look at Hunter. "Mama, Hunter is not 'the help.' He's the freaking star of the New Orleans Fire, and he's being kind enough to help you out with your plumbing problems. Please apologize to him. Now."

Mama shakes her head at me, but she turns to Hunter, who's staring at me. His expression has softened, and suddenly it's back to him and me against the world.

"Hunter, I apologize for my rudeness," Mama says stiffly. "My daughter has always brought out the worst in me."

Hunter doesn't take his eyes off me when he says, "On the contrary, I think your daughter has always shown off the best of both you and your husband."

Mama actually giggles. "Yes, and did you know? Winter still has her sights set on the lead in Summerset Nights. That's her dream role, isn't it, sugar?"

I dig my heels in the ground and nod. "Yes. Hunter knows this already. That role has been my dream since I was a little girl."

Hunter nods at me. "I remember," he says softly in a way I know was meant only for me.

"I'm surprised you haven't been offered the role yet, Winter," Mama says, somehow managing to make me feel at fault.

"New York City has a lot of talent," I say like I've said so many times before. "One day, maybe I'll get lucky."

"You should have seen her in Seasonal Bliss," Mama says to Hunter. "My Winter stole the show! The audience gave her two standing ovations."

"Mama." I tilt my head at Hunter in apology. "Hunter didn't have time to go to New York to see a show. He's got games nearly every night. Being a professional athlete isn't easy, and he's doing amazing."

"Just like you are, Win." With one last look at me, Hunter turns away to clean up and put his tools away.

"I'll start bringing my stuff out to your truck," I say as I rush downstairs to grab a suitcase.

CHAPTER SEVEN

Driving my mom's car, I follow Hunter through New Orleans, barely noticing where I am but making sure I stick close behind him so I don't get lost. With everything that's changed over the last forty-eight hours, my thoughts are jumbled.

Hunter Storm was my first real crush. But it was unresolved. We never slept together, although we almost did. And then I left New Orleans, and we stopped being friends and became... nothing at all. Moving away to pursue my dreams didn't make us lose each other. But life, and time, did.

We didn't ever date, anyway. We weren't like normal couples. Since grade school, we hung out, and as teenagers, we sometimes crossed the line.

We flirted relentlessly with one another through high school, but then we always found a way to ignore the fire between us.

That fire is still there, though. And God help me, I don't want to pretend anymore.

———

An hour later, Hunter brings the last of my bags into his guest suite.

And just like that, I've moved in.

"Looks like you've officially got yourself a human house-mate," I say with a smile. "I promise to take good care of Theo."

"I know you will." He gives me a nod. "I'm off to practice."

"Okay. Have fun."

He pauses in the doorway. "I signed a six-month contract with the pet sitting agency," he says, leaning against my doorjamb.

"Right. Six months."

"So." He settles in more against the door frame. "Does that mean you're returning to Broadway in six months?"

I clench my hands into balls at my sides. "That's the plan."

His gaze on me feels as hot as the sun. It's like he can see right through me.

Desperate to change the subject, I say in a rush of words, "I'm meeting Ashley and Peyton at The Riverway tonight. I think Oliver will be there. Why don't you join us after practice if you're up for it?"

"Sure. I can do that."

"Great." I remember my car. "Shit! I left my mother's car in the street while we unpacked the truck. I need to move it."

"I'll come with you."

———

Hunter

All these years, and I never once saw Winter Allen. Now I can't get away from her. And I don't want to.

We walk together down my short driveway and over to her mother's BMW that's parked by the curb. I wait for Winter to unlock the doors before getting into the shotgun seat.

I'm still wound up from our argument at her parents' house earlier and by the way Winter's body felt when I put my hands on her. I haven't touched Winter in ages, and the last two times we've touched, my whole body fucking lit up. I could have taken her against the bathroom wall right then and there. And if her mother hadn't come upstairs, I might have gone for it.

"So your mama's BMW fetish is still going strong, I take it."

"Of course." Winter puts the key in the ignition, and I try to ignore how every little movement she makes turns me on. "My mother can be counted on to never change. Always wanting me to be the best, and never happy with what I achieve."

She jerks her head over to me after she says it, and I know she didn't mean for all that to come out of her mouth. She nearly drives right past my house in her distraction, but I gesture to the left, and she veers into the driveway at the last moment.

"Shit."

I bite back a grin. "You seem a little out of it. Are you tired from being woken up early?" I ask her as we get out of the car. "You could take a nap with Theo. Like human-cat bonding time."

"Maybe I will." She flicks her gaze over to me. "If you didn't have practice, I'd invite you to join us."

My dick hardens immediately. "Is that right?" As we step inside my house, I pause in the doorway, causing Winter to bump into my side. Which was exactly my plan.

I reach out and wrap my arm around her waist. "Can I take you up on your offer another time?"

She leans into my side. "Yes. But you shouldn't be late for practice. So go. Score lots of goals."

I chuckle. "It's practice, babe. I save my scoring for the real thing."

She elbows me playfully. "Ha, ha. Just go do your thing. I'll see you tonight."

I'm still smiling as I get into my truck.

And as I drive through the city to the stadium.

And it's all because of Winter.

Who I can't hook up with. One, because she's my house-mate, and two, because she's Winter. We were always fire and gasoline. And judging by our fight earlier, nothing's changed.

I need to stay focused on getting out of my slump, not fantasizing over a woman who's leaving in six months and who I can't be with anyway.

I'm fucked.

CHAPTER EIGHT

Winter

Wearing an ankle-length black skirt, aqua wraparound sweater, and strappy, open-toed shoes, I hustle into The Riverway.

"Winter!!!" Peyton calls out as she throws her arms around me. "I'm so glad you made it!"

Before I can answer her, Ashley Hill makes it a three-way hug. "Yay, the three of us together again!"

I pull back and smile at them. Peyton and Ashley, my two best girlfriends since we were in diapers.

No matter how far away I feel from my old life, Peyton and Ashley never fade into the past. They've been on my side from the beginning, and I know they always will be.

Peyton's cream shirt contrasts with her dark hair perfectly, and Ashley's purple tie-dye shirt and short skirt look great against her hazel eyes and auburn shoulder-length bob. I'm taller than both of them, and my naturally slim stature contrasts with their curvier figures. I always envied them their curves, and they wanted to be tall and thin. It's human nature, I think, to want what we can't have.

"We've got company tonight," Peyton says. "Scott and Oliver are here. Already drinking."

I laugh. "I could use a drink or two myself, to be honest. Maybe we should join them and get good and drunk."

"Oh my God, let's do it." Ashley grabs my hand and pulls me toward the back table. "I want to know everything that's going on with you. I feel like we haven't really talked since you became a star!"

Peyton walks on my other side. "Ash and I sat in the front row at your show on Broadway and just kept poking each other, saying, 'Can you believe that's our best friend up there?' I remember when your mother had you auditioning for that baby commercial. Seems like just yesterday."

Ashley and I look at her and burst out laughing. "You do not remember that!" Ashley says. "You were a baby, too!"

Peyton shrugs. "It's a legendary story around here. I feel like I remember it personally."

Peyton's big brother, Oliver, rushes me when I reach the table. He picks me up, and her boyfriend, Scott, hands me a beer while I beg for Oliver to put me down.

"Haven't seen you in forever, Ms. Allen." He kisses my cheek, and as he returns me to the ground, Scott greets me before Ashley wraps her arms around me in another hug.

"Welcome home," she says to me quietly. "I know you didn't want to leave Manhattan, but maybe the time away will be good for you."

I look into her hazel eyes, nearly the same color as Peyton's but with a dash more pain. Ashley would understand what I'm going through. My situation was different than hers, but we both know what it's like to deal with abuse. I trust her. I just don't want to talk to anyone about what happened to me.

We all sit down, and I take a big sip of my beer.

"And guess who we texted?" Oliver says with a sideways glance at me. "Our hockey friend."

Peyton turns on Oliver. "You should have known better than

that! No inviting Hunter here tonight. I went over this with you!"

I calmly lean back against my chair. "It's fine."

Oliver points at me. "See, Win's okay with it. The group of us have known each other our whole lives. And Winter's here for six months—I think she and Hunt should hang out. We all know you two ended on a sour note, but that was years ago."

Peyton smothers a laugh. Obviously, Blaire didn't tell her husband what she and Peyton and I chatted about yesterday.

And I don't tell the table the truth—I've not only already seen Hunter Storm but I'm now living with him. I figure I'll wait until he arrives, and we can surprise them together.

"He said he's coming here?" I ask Oliver.

He nods. "On his way."

Oliver and Scott start chatting about the Fire and how Oliver thinks they have a great chance to win it all this year.

"Of course, not if his brothers have something to say about it out in Montana." Oliver chuckles. "Plus, Declan Wild for the Kings is a fucking stud."

"He's been a star for years," Peyton says.

"I know, but this season he's really on a roll," Oliver says. "Along with Jared and Max, the Kings could present a real challenge for the title."

"We can handle them." Hunter's deep voice comes from directly behind me.

His hand lightly touches my shoulder and sends shivers down my spine.

Four heads turn to look at me.

I will my pounding heart to relax, and I put on what I hope looks like a casual smile as Hunter grabs a chair and pushes it in between me and Oliver.

His arm is around me before I can speak. "Hey, Princess."

I turn to face him. His green eyes are focused on me like nobody else is at the table. I forgot how good it felt to be

noticed like this. Because nobody's ever noticed me—the real me
—the way Hunter Storm has.

"Hi, Hunt."

I lean in and kiss his cheek. He's not expecting that, and
honestly, neither was I. I just can't help myself around him—it's
like his body's begging for me to touch him.

The scent of his aftershave and the feel of his skin against my
lips overwhelm me. I try to pull back quickly, but his hand goes
around my neck, and before I know it, he's kissing me back. Just
on the cheek, but butterflies dance in my stomach.

We let go of each other then and turn back to the table like
nothing just happened.

Everyone's staring at us, and Ashley's eyes are saucer-wide.
"What—I mean, you two haven't seen each other in years, and
you haven't exactly wanted to stay in contact. So how did this—
kissing and touching—happen?"

Hunter quirks an eyebrow. "I see your nosiness hasn't ebbed
over the years, Ash."

I elbow him in the ribs. "Don't be rude. Hunter and I ran
into each other yesterday."

Ashley gasps. "Was it a planned meeting or spontaneous?"

Peyton giggles next to me. "How are you going to field this
question?" she murmurs so only I can hear.

Oliver furrows his brow at Hunter. "You didn't say a word in
your text. Not even a whisper."

"I didn't realize Winter and I were supposed to report everything back to y'all," Hunter says. "Yes, I had a Winter Allen
sighting yesterday when she agreed to pet sit Theo."

"Ohhh," Ashley says. "Coincidence or planned?"

"Coincidence," I say. "I applied for the job, and it turned out
to be Hunter. Small world." I put my hand on his arm. "We're
going to be housemates."

The laughter that breaks out at our table is so loud people
look over.

"You two—" Oliver points from Hunter to me. "Are going to live together?"

"Yes." I keep my hand on Hunter's arm. "I moved in today."

Ashley smiles at me happily. "I think this is great news." She holds up her glass of wine. "You two will have so much time to reconnect!"

Hunter shakes his head. "Fucking nosy people."

Everyone relaxes, and all of us but Hunter proceed to finish our drinks. And then we order more. And more.

We talk about high school and grade school, and they catch me up on all the gossip I've missed out on over the years. It's so nice not to talk about auditions and the latest fad diet or the best way to baby your voice leading up to a performance. I get to be a person again, and my whole body relaxes.

Hunter and I don't touch again for the remainder of the night. But I'm always aware of him—of his hand near mine when I reach for my beer, of his absence when a pretty redhead beckons to him from the bar and he goes and speaks to her. He's not gone for long, and he doesn't act flirty with her, but I hate the stab of jealousy in my chest as I watch them from the table. I need to get used to seeing him with other women because I can't give him anything that he wants or deserves.

"Who was that?" I ask him when he returns. "An old girlfriend?"

His mouth lifts in a half-smile. "Nope. I don't have those."

"Girlfriends?"

"Right. She's a friend of Cathy, and she wanted an autograph for her son. He's six."

"Do you mind that? Always being on the job in a sense?"

He shrugs. "I don't mind. Especially when they're our fans and not the other team's. What about you? Do you mind the fame?"

I take a large sip of beer. "I don't get recognized much. Some, but not a lot." *And I don't enjoy it.*

Hunter doesn't miss a thing. "You don't like it, though."

I swallow. "Not like I thought I would."

"How come?" he asks me curiously.

"You know, I've been asking myself that same question. I'm not sure."

"Maybe you just need a break."

"Everyone keeps saying that," I say. "And maybe they're right."

I'm far past buzzed when someone taps me on the shoulder. "Winter Allen?" a smiling blond girl says. "I saw you in Seasonal Bliss—can I get your picture, please?"

Hunter catches my eye. When I nod, he takes the girl's phone from her extended hand and snaps a quick picture of her beaming next to me.

Five minutes later, an older woman approaches. "My daughter just got your photo. Would you mind very much taking a quick one with me?"

I feel like I'm floating up out of my body when I say yes. Almost like I'm watching the whole scene from the ceiling.

"We flew to New York and saw you perform," she confides. "My daughter wants to be a singer someday. You're her idol."

"Thank you."

Hunter whispers in my ear that he'll be right back. I watch him go up to the bar and gesture to Ike.

Peyton takes advantage of the moment to slip into Hunter's empty chair. "I think you've got a secret," she says.

I whip my head over to her. "What do you mean?"

I'm pretty drunk, but Peyton's really drunk. So drunk that she doesn't notice my obvious panic. "You and Hunter. Fill me in. What made you decide to keep the job?"

Ashley squats down next to us as she returns from the restroom. "Yeah. Spill it, Allen. Seriously, what are the odds that you'd become Hunter's housemate?"

"Pretty slim," I admit. "I think he was relieved in a way that someone he knew showed up at the door. You know how private he is."

"He always was," Peyton says. "You and he made the perfect private pair, Winter. But living together? Do you think that will be weird?"

She and Ashley look at me expectantly, their mouths partially open and their eyes bright.

"I don't know," I say. "Nothing romantic has happened."

My two girlfriends both visibly deflate in front of my eyes.

Then they try to cover.

"Oh," Peyton says. "Well, that makes sense, of course. I mean, you two have a difficult history, and...and..."

Ashley jumps in to help. "And you're just so hot and stormy together, which would make a peaceful home life challenging if you started being more than friends. Hunter's also a commitment-phobe, and I know you moved on from him long ago..."

"I meant that nothing romantic has happened—*yet*," I blurt out.

Why the hell did I just say that? God, I'm definitely drunk.

Silence. Before—

Loud squeals, hugs and "oh my God," and "this is going to be so much fun."

"No, wait!" I shake my head. "Darn beer. I didn't phrase that right. Nothing is going to happen between Hunter Storm and me. Nothing but a few months of possible friendship and polite..." I can't remember what I meant to say. "What's the word? I can't remember my words. How drunk am I?"

"I think you mean you want sex with Hunter," Ashley says. "Is that what you mean? Sex?"

"Sex." Peyton nods. "I love sex."

"Oh God, me too." Ashley sighs. "I always have casual sex. But I think sometime I want the real kind of sex. You know, the type that lasts. Like you and Scott have, Peyton."

Peyton claps her hands. "Yay! You just made a resolution for love!"

"I did?" Ashley wrinkles her nose. "Isn't that just for New Year's?"

"Hey!" I snap my fingers in front of their faces. "Help me find the word I can't remember. It's not sex—it's the opposite. Like non-sex."

"Companionship?" Ashley suggests.

I point at her. "Genius. Yes, that's the word: companionship. Hunter Storm and I will have companionship in his townhouse. And, that's it."

"Yay for companionship!" Ashley says.

I smile at them. "I've missed you girls sooo much. I love you, and even though I'm drunk, I really do mean it."

"We love you too." Peyton and Ashley hug me, and for the first time since I moved home, I feel at peace.

When Hunter returns to our table, I ask him what he and Ike were talking about. "I thought I saw you guys look over at me," I say.

"I just told him you deserved to enjoy a night out without anyone asking for autographs or selfies. He said he'd make sure you got your privacy."

I stare at him. I can't believe he did that for me.

"Win?" He furrows his brows. "Did I overstep? I'm sorry. I thought you wanted..."

"I did. I do." I smile at him. "That was so incredibly thoughtful of you. Thank you."

"Anything for you, Princess." He says it so quietly I have to strain to hear him.

———

When Ike calls out closing time, Hunter turns to me. "If you took a cab, I'll drive us home."

"I did. You drove here?" I say.

"Keeps me from drinking when I have a big game the next night," he says.

I hug everyone else good night, and Ashley, Peyton, and I make plans to go to Hunter's game tomorrow night.

We're all walking to the door when I have the feeling somebody's watching me.

I glance back at the bar.

A man has swiveled on his stool so he can follow me with his gaze as I walk. I stop in my tracks and look at him.

He smiles and waves in a flirty way then gestures to his drink.

"Let me buy you one," he mouths.

I don't know him. I *know* I don't know him, and over the last year, I've gotten used to being recognized for my work. But something in his face looks eerily familiar; he reminds me of—

"Shit." The word comes out of my mouth too loudly and unexpectedly.

Hunter's immediately by my side. "What is it?"

The blood drains from my face as I point a shaky finger at the man. "He…"

"What? Did he say something to you?" Hunter's got his arm around me now and he's staring hard at the bar. "Tell me what he did, Winter. I'll go make sure he never does it again."

I shake my head. "I have to go home. Please take me home."

Hunter turns me toward the door. "Okay."

———

I don't think any of the others noticed what happened as we were leaving, and Hunter doesn't say anything in front of them. But he helps me with my seat belt after I climb into the front seat, and I can feel his gaze on me every time we hit a stoplight.

I spend the time focusing on my breathing like the therapist said to do.

Long breath in through the nose, longer breath out through the mouth. Just relax. I'll be okay. This too shall pass.

When we reach Hunter's place, he parks next to my mother's BMW and shuts off the engine.

"I'll help you inside," he says as he opens his door.

By the time he makes it around to my side, I'm already out of his truck and heading for the front door.

Hunter takes a hold of my arm and walks with me. Once we're inside and I go to disappear into my suite, he says my name quietly.

I look up into his emerald eyes. "I'm fine. I just need to sleep."

"You're not fine. You're white as a sheet. Let me help you."

I don't fight him, partly because I'm so drunk and partly because I don't want to be alone. Theo scampers out from wherever he was and rubs his body against my legs.

I scoop him up into my arms and bury my face in his soft fur. "Hi, buddy. You want to sleep with me tonight?" I look up at Hunter, who's watching us. "Is that okay with you?"

His eyes fill with affection. "Of course. I don't let him sleep on my bed."

"Why not?"

"I need to make sure I get uninterrupted sleep during the season. So he's not allowed in my room."

"You're such a strict daddy," I tease him.

He chuckles and leads me into the kitchen. I put Theo down, but he stays close to me as Hunter gets me a bottled water. Then he makes me my favorite hangover remedy—a peanut butter and jelly sandwich.

"You remembered," I say softly as he hands it to me.

"Of course I do." His hand goes to the small of my back as he guides me toward the guest suite.

Theo happily follows.

When we reach the bedroom, I take Hunter's hand in mine and pull him into my room. I sit cross-legged on my bed up by the pillows, and Theo jumps up to join me. Hunter takes a seat at the end.

I devour my sandwich and drink half the bottle of water. Then we look at each other in silence. Until Hunter breaks it.

"What's going on, Princess?"

His eyes lock with mine, and I can't avoid his piercing gaze. But I can't give him what he's looking for.

I give a little shrug. "I don't want to talk about it. Is that a sufficient answer? Because it's all you're going to get out of me on the subject."

"All I'm going to get out of you tonight or forever?" he asks me.

"Forever." I tighten my hands into fists on my lap and lift my chin defiantly.

He sighs and runs a hand through his dark hair, causing the errant wavy lock to fall over his forehead again. He pushes it out of his face impatiently, and I resist the urge to do it for him, to brush it off his forehead tenderly and then kiss him as hard as I can.

"Winter, I won't push you. But just know that I can't help you if you won't let me. And you look like you need some help." He stands up. "You coming to the game tomorrow night?"

I nod. "Can't wait."

"I'll be sure to score a goal for you." He kisses my head so quickly I almost think I imagined it. "See you in the morning, Princess."

He leaves, shutting the door behind him.

CHAPTER NINE

Hunter

"Hey." Liam lets me into his house the next afternoon. It's five hours before our big game. His dark hair is damp from the shower, and he's got a towel around his neck. "Give me ten minutes to finish up."

"No problem. We've got some time." I break into a smile as Cathy comes into the living room carrying Lulu.

My niece starts wriggling in her mama's arms and sticking out her hands toward me.

I walk closer and kiss her on the cheek, and she giggles. With her blond hair and big blue eyes, she's the cutest freaking kid I've ever seen.

"Hi, sweetheart," I say to her. "How are you?"

"She's been cranky all morning." Cathy sighs. "This is the first time she's acted happy. She's got a serious crush on her Uncle Hunter."

"Are you going to watch the game?" I ask Lulu. "Your daddy and I are playing our rival team tonight. Between you and me, we're definitely going to win."

"God, you better beat Montana," Cathy says. "Liam's been talking about this game against the Wild Kings all season."

"That's because our two brothers are on the team and nothing would give us more pleasure than to kick their butts," Liam says as he comes out of the bedroom. "Right, Hunt? You ready for tonight?"

"More than ready," I say seriously. "Max and Jared have been giving us shit since they beat us last year on their ice. It's our turn now."

"Damn right." Liam reaches for his bag and hugs Cathy and Lulu. "See you after the game. Love you."

I try not to notice the fact that Cathy pulls back from my brother's kiss, or the eye roll she gives him when he whispers something in her ear.

I wave goodbye to her and kiss Lulu on the head. "See you soon, baby girl."

Liam and I leave the house and get into my truck. We drive for about ten minutes before I say what's on my mind.

"What's up with you and Cath?"

Long exhale followed by a curse before he says, "Stay out of it, Hunt."

"Is everything okay?" I press. "I'm just checking in. Seemed like there was some tension."

"None more than usual." I can feel his hard glare even though I'm not looking at him. "You'll understand when you have a kid. It's tough."

"I'm sure it is. Why don't you two go on a date night? I can babysit whenever you need."

He goes silent, and I'm sure he's going to ignore my offer. My oldest brother is a pain in the ass, but he's got his reasons. He and Cathy were high school sweethearts, yet I never thought they'd marry. Something always seemed off between them, but when she got pregnant unexpectedly, they decided to tie the knot. It was none of my business, though I worried they were marrying for the wrong reasons.

"Standing offer if you ever need the help," I say.

He waits until I'm pulling into the hockey arena before he says, "You free tomorrow night?"

"Sure." I turn off the truck, and we step out.

He punches my arm. "Thanks, Hunt."

———

Sometimes, a game goes well. Sometimes, it's shit.

And sometimes, on rare nights, it goes exactly how you would draw it up in your dreams.

Tonight is one of those games.

The Montana Wild Kings come into New Orleans, and we're ready for them.

And I'm more than ready to get out of my damn slump.

During warm-ups, I look up into the stands where I know Winter will be.

There she is, sitting next to Peyton and Ashley. I raise my stick in greeting, and Winter waves back.

"Hey!" Murph skates over to me and nearly checks me into the boards. "Don't get distracted, remember? I still can't believe your pet sitter is your fucking ex!"

"She won't distract me," I assure him. "And she's not my ex."

Not exactly.

"Oh, yeah? Winter Allen and you may not have officially dated, but come on, man. Your history isn't exactly platonic. And what's she doing right now?" he says. "She's giving you that flirty-as-fuck wave. For all you know, she's rooting for the other team!"

I laugh. "Winter's on our side, Murph. Chill the hell out, will you? I'm coming out of my slump tonight. I can feel it."

As if to prove my point, I tap the puck at my feet, and with a short wind-up, slap that sucker twenty feet into the net. Right past the goalie's outstretched glove.

Coach whistles from the bench. "Looking better, Hunt! Let's keep it up!"

I turn to Murph. "Talk to me after the game if you don't believe me now."

————

Winter

It's been so long—too long—since I've watched Hunter play hockey in person. His games have been my guilty secret since he hit the pros, but I haven't been to a game since high school. Scott, Peyton, Ashley, and I are sitting at center ice with an amazing view of the game. Scott's got his arm around Peyton, and Ashley's flirting with the two guys on her other side while I sit and watch Hunter warm up with his teammates.

I'm so excited, and having Peyton and Ash with me brings back a lot of memories.

"Remember how we'd have to drive to Baton Rouge to watch him and his brothers play?" I laugh. "A bunch of southern boys playing ice hockey."

"I know. It's amazing the four of them were able to make the pros," Ashley says.

"Their dad saved up for them to travel north and go to hockey camps every summer," I say. "He took out a second mortgage on his house in order to afford their training, and it ended up paying off."

"Mr. Storm would be flipping out to see a professional team in New Orleans," Peyton says. "I hope they last."

"It's been three years now, which is three years longer than I would have thought it would stick." I glance around at the arena. "And it's packed tonight."

"It is." Ashley shrugs. "People come to socialize and relax. I don't know if they really understand the sport yet. It's growing on them, though."

"What they need is for the Fire to win a championship," Scott says. "That would increase interest in the sport around here."

"The city would go nuts if that happens," Peyton agrees.

We stand and cheer for the player introductions.

Then, the game starts.

And I'm immediately transfixed.

Unlike my two best friends.

Like they used to do in high school, Peyton and Ashley tune the game out as they get into a long chat across my lap. First, it's something about Peyton's shoe business. They move on to Ashley's job as social media expert for a marketing and PR firm. She's advertising new wedding accessories right now, and she talks about flash gold temporary tattoos and how fast they're selling. I miss the rest of their conversation because I'm too busy watching Hunter.

He assists on New Orleans's first goal and helps kill a power play by Montana. Then, he splits two defenders on a breakaway and slides the puck past the flailing goalie.

I'm screaming so loudly I know I'll be hoarse later.

I'm certainly no hockey expert, but I've been following Hunter's career for years, and even I know when somebody's on fire. Hunter's freaking hot tonight, and he knows it. After he scores a second goal on a one-timer from the right circle, he punches his stick in the air and points to where we're sitting. I can't help the smile that breaks out on my face.

And when he slams a defender into the boards right in front of us, I stand up and shout.

"Go, Hunt!"

As I sit back down, Scott chuckles.

"Didn't know you were such a cheerleader," he says. "Your enthusiasm's infectious."

Ashley and Peyton are grinning at me.

"What?" I stick out my tongue at them. "I'm rooting for the Fire. That's all."

"Uh-huh." Peyton takes my hand in hers and squeezes it. "It's good to see you happy, Win. We've been worried about you."

"What do you mean?" I ask her. "I'm okay."

Ashley narrows her eyes. "Are you?"

Peyton lets go of my hand as Ashley keeps talking.

"Something's different with you," she says quietly.

I keep my eyes on the ice. "I'm not sure what you're talking about."

"I mean, the last bunch of times we've talked on the phone, you've seemed sadder than usual. But, you've looked happier tonight. And I don't know, you and Hunter last night...you two couldn't have hung out like that before."

"We hung out in high school."

"You fought in high school," Peyton says. "Then, you'd hook up. Then, you'd fight again. Obviously, you two have chemistry for days, but you couldn't handle it when you were young." She puts her hand on my arm. "Maybe it was too big for teenagers to process, you know?"

"Hunter is a force of nature," I admit. "He could light a place on fire with his energy." *I think maybe that scared me. It still does.*

"And you take over a room full of people with yours." Peyton laughs. "You two are so alike, actually. You're used to being in front of thousands of people, but you fear intimacy."

I'm not sure what to say to that. I'm actually not comfortable in either situation.

I turn to Peyton, deciding to ask the question that's been on my mind since I moved back home.

"Do you think the police will ever re-open Mr. Storm's murder case?" I ask.

"Not without a lead." She frowns. "It sucks, but some criminals are never caught."

No. Sometimes they're not.

But sometimes, the stars align. Even if you weren't the one who turned them in, sometimes the bad guy does have to pay for what he did. I know that firsthand.

I wonder if Hunter's bad guy will ever have to suffer the way he made the Storm family.

"You okay?" Ashley gives me a closer look.

I nod quickly, feeling like she can see right through me. There's nothing like old friends—they cut right through the bullshit. "Fine."

I return my attention to the game. As I watch Hunter steal the puck away from a defender and take off down the ice, I forget everything but him.

He passes the puck to Liam, who pulls up on the left wing close to the goal. He maintains possession of the puck with two players between him and the net. I lose sight of Hunter until all of a sudden, he appears from behind the net just as Liam flicks the puck over to him, and Hunter slots it in with his stick.

The puck moves so fast I don't realize it's a goal until Liam and Hunter start cheering and getting mobbed by their teammates.

My throat burns as I scream. Scott kisses Peyton, Ashley and I hug each other, and the entire arena stands and cheers as time runs out.

Peyton's right. I haven't had this much fun in ages.

"Let's go wait for Hunter and Liam so we can congratulate them," Ashley says.

Peyton and I look at her. "You mean, so you can say hi to Jared," I tease her.

Ashley flushes red. "Jared and I are just friends."

Peyton snorts with laughter. "Right."

Ashley grabs my hand. "Come with me. Unless you want Hunter to be surrounded by puck bunnies instead."

I flush with heat. Jealous? No doubt.

"Okay," I say. "Let's go wait for them."

CHAPTER TEN

Ashley wasn't kidding about the puck bunnies.

The line-up of women waiting for the New Orleans and Montana players to come out of the locker rooms takes up the entire width of the corridor and spills down the hallway.

Peyton and Scott take one look at the crowd of people and decide to go home.

"They were smart," I say to Ashley as we stand at the back of the pack. "What are we doing here again? I can just see Hunter at home later."

Ashley shakes her head. "That's no fun! All the Storm brothers are back together for a night—you think they're not going to go out and party? Let's join them!"

"Like old times?" I say, remembering high school and some of the nights we all spent together.

"Exactly." Just as she says it, the girls in front of us start screaming.

I can't see much, and I'm being jostled, but I catch a glimpse of a security guard directing everyone to stand back.

Several more security guards step out and clear the way further until there's a tunnel in the center of the crowd. The door to the visiting locker room opens up, and players start filing out.

Declan Wild strides out first with a couple of his teammates. Crap, he's gorgeous. Anyone with eyes would notice him. Dark hair and the most intense gray eyes, coupled with a gray suit that looks like it cost a fortune. Declan's been a superstar for a long time, and he carries himself that way. He's confident, sure of himself, and he doesn't look around at a single fan no matter how much they scream.

"He's so damn hot," Ashley whispers.

"For sure," I say back.

"I can't believe he grew up in Louisiana," she says. "I wish he'd gone to school in New Orleans so I could have crushed on him."

I laugh. "He's older than us, Ash. He wouldn't have been close to the same grade anyway. But I think Hunter said that the Wild family lived a couple of hours outside of the city."

"Well, that's a damn shame," she says. "Because sweet Lord, is he fine to look at."

The two teammates walking with Declan are also easy on the eyes. Tex Williams and Arch Morrison—both of them smirk at the women calling to them, and Tex stops to take a couple of selfies. Arch signs a woman's shirt, and a hat, and…

"Panties?" Ashley says incredulously as the woman holds up a pink pair of lacy underwear to Arch. "I hope she washed them first."

While we're giggling, Jared and Max Storm come out of the locker room.

And the women start screaming all over again.

Fraternal twins, Jared and Max are the two middle Storm brothers with Jared being a few minutes older. All four boys are dark-haired, but Jared and Max have chocolate brown eyes instead of green.

I can't help but notice the smile on Ashley's face as she stares at Jared.

Both guys take a few selfies with the puck bunnies and sign some shirts and other things. No panties this time, from what I can see. Max keeps his distance from the women, and Jared grins and makes friendly small talk the entire time.

"Those two are so damn different," Ashley whispers to me. "Max can't be bothered to give any woman the time of day, and Jared gives them exactly what they want."

"I don't know about that," I say. "Jared's just putting on a show."

As they wave goodbye to the fans, both guys flash megawatt smiles like they're loving the attention. Their smiles aren't real, though, and they remind me of myself after a performance.

Of course, I know they appreciate the support; I also know they want to get away from the crowds. Like Ashley says, Max is particularly reclusive; I've never even heard of him dating anyone. And Jared is more of a flirt, although he and Ashley have a mysterious history that Peyton and I have never been able to figure out.

Security doesn't allow anyone to get out of control, and before long, Jared and Max are standing right in front of Ashley and me.

"Holy crap." Jared stops short, and this time, a genuine smile crosses his face. "My hometown girls." He puts a huge muscled arm around each of us. "So good to see you." He whispers something I can't hear into Ashley's ear.

"You too." I smile over at Max, who nods his head in greeting.

"Heard you were back in town, Win," he says to me in his typical gruff tone. "Maybe you can keep my brother in line."

"Who, Hunter?" I raise my eyebrows. "I don't think Hunter likes being kept in line."

"I think he's been known to make an exception a time or two," he says cryptically with a wink at me.

Like I can feel Hunter's presence, I look around Max at the

gap in the crowd. Sure enough, the door to the Fire locker room has opened, and the team is walking out.

The screams increase about tenfold to what they were for the Wild Kings, and I can't help from smiling as I catch sight of Hunter. He's with Liam, plus another teammate that I recognize as Dean Harris, along with Camden "Murph" Murphy. Murph went to school with all of us, and he was inseparable with the Storms.

Hunter can't possibly see me from this angle, but he's walking quickly down the corridor, and he'll be upon us in a matter of seconds. That is until a woman jumps the barricade and hurls her body against his.

Hunter's not expecting it, and he lurches backward momentarily before regaining his balance.

Security reacts swiftly, but not before the woman has wrapped her arms around Hunter's neck and is headed for his mouth with her own.

He twists his head to avoid the kiss and shoves her off of him. The guard pins her arms behind her and carries her off.

I'm frozen in place as I watch.

"Some people don't know the words personal space," Ashley mutters.

Hunter pushes past the security guard, and as he looks up, I step forward.

He sees me. A crooked grin takes over his face, the kind of smile that drives women wild. The kind of smile that always got us into trouble. While I'm still processing what it means that he's giving me that look right now, he heads straight for me.

I expect him to stop when he reaches me and maybe crack an awkward joke about what just happened when the crazy fan accosted him.

What I don't expect is for him to pick me up in his arms and kiss the hell out of me.

Oh. My. God.

I forgot how good it felt to kiss Hunter. So good. So right, the way his lips feel against mine. The way my body melds into his.

The kiss doesn't last long, but there's definitely tongue. And tenderness. And I don't want it to stop.

I haven't kissed Hunter Storm in ten years, and no one since has come close to...*that*. The way he fits with me. The urgency and gentleness.

He pulls back after a few seconds, and I read the apology in his eyes. He immediately lets me down to the ground like he's worried he overstepped.

He would have no way of knowing this, but I haven't kissed anyone since I was attacked six months ago. I thought I was broken. No one has even made me contemplate anything sexual until I moved back to New Orleans and ended up on Hunter's front porch.

I was so sure I'd feel different, like that asshole who took something from me without my permission had permanently changed me. I've felt so shut down, so numb inside, and I was terrified I'd never feel turned on again. But that kiss just now...it liberated me a little bit. And I want to feel all the way freed.

I stare up at Hunter while his brothers slap him on the back and joke with him about keeping things PG when we're out in public.

He's barely answering them because he's too busy staring back at me. When he mouths "sorry" to me, I realize he's misread my reaction.

I shake my head almost imperceptibly to try to let him know I'm fine, but we don't have time to communicate any more than that because Dean and Murph insist that we all go to The Riverway.

Soon, we're piling into Liam and Hunter's trucks. I end up in the back of Hunter's truck with Ashley squeezed in next to me and Jared on her other side.

"What was that between you and Hunter?" she manages to whisper in my ear.

"I was as surprised as you," I whisper back.

"Peyton is going to be so mad she missed it. God, that was a hot kiss, Win!"

It was. It was so. Damn. Hot.

CHAPTER ELEVEN

The Riverway is crowded, and Ashley drags me up to the bar to chat with Blaire about the game. Really, I think she's dying for me to tell her about my kiss with Hunter.

I don't say anything, though, and Ashley manages to keep her mouth shut. She does grab my arm and squeal when Blaire asks how Hunter played in the game, but as soon as the four Storm brothers, plus Dean and Murph, join us, Ashley gets distracted by Jared.

"What's up with those two?" Hunter says in my ear.

I glance at Ashley giggling at something Jared said to her. He's completely focused on her.

"I think they had a thing for each other in high school," I say. "Don't you remember?"

Hunter takes a sip of his beer. "Jared never said anything."

I laugh. "That doesn't mean it's not true. Jared never shares his feelings on many subjects."

"True." He leans in closer. "Speaking of, we need to talk."

I bite my lip. "I know. But not here."

"Later," he murmurs in a low voice filled with promise.

I suppress a shiver. I hope I know what I'm doing.

"Hey!" Jared calls out.

His gaze is fixed over my shoulder, and I whip around.

Declan Wild is here. His ball cap is pulled low over his face, and he's standing in the darkest corner of the bar. It's clear he doesn't want the attention, but his teammates don't seem to be on the same page. Tex Williams and Arch Morrison stand calmly in the center of the attention all three are already getting.

The Storm brothers are pretty famous in the world of hockey. But Declan Wild is a modern-day Wayne Gretzky, and he's from Louisiana too, which makes him all the more interesting to the patrons of the bar.

"Welcome home, Mr. Wild!" A roar comes up from the crowd.

Declan gives an appreciative nod and hand wave before sinking into the nearest seat. His perfect jawline is tensed, and his cheeks are flushed. Tex and Arch take seats at the same table with him, and all three bend their heads together in conversation.

"I feel bad for him," I say out loud.

Hunter gives me a look.

"What?" I say to him. "I do."

Ashley overhears me. "I do too, Win. Poor guy just wants some privacy. How could he possibly enjoy himself when he goes out?"

"Oh, for Christ's sake," Jared says. "Are you two serious right now? You feel sorry for one of the biggest stars this sport has ever seen? A guy who had an eight-figure, fully-guaranteed contract he just played out with the Denver Alphas, not to mention his endless endorsement deals? Declan Wild is a great guy, but to say you feel sorry for him is taking it too far."

"You're just jealous." Ashley twirls a lock of auburn hair with her finger and sticks out her tongue at him. "So sad to be jealous of such a great guy like you said."

Jared glares at her as she continues to tangle her hair around her finger and smile at him teasingly. Jared looks like he's either going to fight with her or kiss her, and Ashley doesn't seem to be sure which option she'd choose.

"What do you think?" Hunter says in my ear. "Do you feel sorry for Wild?"

I glance over at Declan but draw back in surprise when I realize he's coming this way.

"Um..." I wave my hands at Ashley.

She looks at me with her eyebrows raised. Until she sees who's coming up behind me.

She gasps and grabs my arm so hard I'm sure I'll find a bruise in the morning.

"Declan Wild!" she says loudly. "What an honor—can we get you a drink?"

Declan's perfect lips twitch as his gaze flicks to her, but he simply shakes his head. "Thanks for the offer, but I'm about to leave. I'm looking for Max," he tells Jared. "Need to see him before I go."

Jared nods, reaches through Liam and Murph, and somehow manages to snag Max by the shoulder. Max is laughing with Dean about something, but he turns around. When he sees Declan standing there amongst us, he immediately gets off his stool and steps over to him.

"Hey, Wild." He offers him his beer. "Have a drink with us."

Declan tries to decline, but Max has already shoved the bottle into his hand, and Ashley's peppering him with questions.

Where in Louisiana did you grow up?

Do you miss the south?

Rumor has it you're going to retire soon. Is it true?

I'm sure he's going to give her some quick lip service answer and get the hell away from us.

Instead, he surprises me.

"I grew up by Covington. I do miss the south sometimes. And as for retirement, I don't make decisions like that mid-season," he says in a deep, sexy voice that I swear my ovaries just responded to with a little leap of joy.

I'm not the only one. Ashley's lips part as she stares up at him, and behind the bar, Blaire freezes in place with a customer's drink in her hand. When I catch her eye, she mouths, "Oh. My. God."

I nod back at her. Yes, Declan Wild's voice matches his gorgeous looks and star status.

And the crazy thing is, Blaire's happily married, I don't want any man but Hunter, and Ashley—whether she'll admit it or not —has a thing for Jared.

So, if Declan Wild can have this kind of an effect on women who *aren't* interested in sleeping with him, I wonder what it will be like for a woman who *does* want him in her bed. My guess is that will be quite the ride.

"Hey." Hunter's eyes flash with amusement as he looks at me. "Did I get this wrong or did you, Blaire, and Ashley all just swoon?"

I tuck my hand in the crook of his elbow and lean my head on his shoulder. "You got it right. We were totally swooning. Because Declan Wild is swoon-worthy."

"So let me get this straight—you're crushing on the star of our rival?"

"No." I beckon to him so his ear is right next to my mouth before I add, "My crushing is reserved for you."

"I like that answer." His hot breath on my skin makes me break out in shivers.

———

We hang out at the Riverway for hours, and it's nice to see Hunter catch up with his brothers. Liam leaves early to get home to his wife and daughter, but the rest of us stay until closing. Jared and Max had gotten permission to stay the night, and they go to Liam's so they can see their niece in the morning. Hunter tells them good night, and the three of them make plans to meet for an early breakfast.

I hug Ashley before Hunter and I head out to his truck. I insist on driving even though he says he only had one beer.

I believe him when he says he's sober, but taking the wheel gives me a sense of purpose on our drive back to his place, where I have a feeling we're going to have some sort of come to Jesus talk.

As soon as we walk into the townhouse, we go find Theo. Turns out he's hungry for a snack, so I feed him while Hunter cleans his litter box. Then, Theo happily settles on the top of his cat tower for a nap in the living room.

And Hunter and I start talking over each other.

"Princess, I'm sorry..." he starts.

"What was that kiss about?" I begin.

He holds up a hand. "I don't know what came over me. That crazy fan was hounding me, and I felt so out of control. Then, I saw you in the crowd, and I just..." He pulls up short and takes a seat on the living room couch.

I follow and sit on the other end of the couch. "You just... what?" I ask him.

His green eyes roam my face for a moment before he speaks.

"I wanted you," he says casually in that way only Hunter Storm can pull off. "I've never stopped wanting you, Winter."

Butterflies roll through my stomach.

I wanted you.

So fucking casual. So Hunter Storm.

And God, I wanted him too. I want him right this very second.

I fist my hands and shove them under my thighs to stop from reaching for him.

"It's been years," I say softly.

"I know how long it's been." He rubs the slight scruff on his jaw. "I've counted the years since you left knowing I fucked it up by not talking things through with you before you moved. And we had that big blow-up over nothing your last night here, which I'm also sorry for."

I shake my head. "You didn't fuck anything up, Hunt. That fight was a two-way street thing. Really, it was just a way for us to make a clean break. We were kids. And we both had big plans. If we'd hung onto what could have been..."

"I get it." His jaw hardens. "I had to sacrifice everything to get where I am. I come from nothing, and hockey was my one shot to make something of myself. For my future. But that doesn't mean I didn't think of you. A lot."

"You know what the truth is?" I can barely get the words out through the lust coursing through me. "I thought of you all the damn time in New York City, Hunter. Every. Single. Day."

He turns his head slowly until his gaze locks with mine. His green eyes darken to the color of a pine forest, and we stare at each other. Three heartbeats pass. Until—

With a low growl, Hunter stands up off the couch and then resettles himself next to me. His mouth lands on mine so fast I should have been surprised again.

But this time, I'm ready for him.

My lips part, and Hunter's hot tongue slides inside.

His hand tangles in my hair, and I ease closer to him.

"Fuck, Winter." He groans into my mouth and kisses me harder.

When one of his hands goes to my breast and the other closes around my waist, it's like I have an out-of-body experience.

I split in half. I want Hunter—that will always be true.

I've survived an attack—that is also true.

And as Hunter and I continue to make out, my two truths are at war with each other.

I'm broken. I'll always be broken.

I pull away from his hands on me.

Desperate for him not to notice, I tug at his shirt until he drags it over his head. And then, I kiss my way down his neck and across his bare, muscled chest. I keep going down his chiseled abs until I reach the waistband of his jeans. Hunter sucks in his breath and mutters my name as I undo the snap and lower the zipper, and then I leave the couch and drop to my knees on the carpet.

Kneeling in between Hunter's legs, I shove my hand inside his boxer briefs and release his massive erection.

"Win..." he says in warning.

But I'm not listening to any warnings to slow down. I'm full steam ahead.

I get my mouth on him, and he jerks against my tongue. I close my mouth tight around his thick length and take as much of him as I can inside me. When he hits the back of my throat, I start gagging.

"Hey." Hunter takes hold of my shoulders and does everything he can to push me off of him. "Winter."

But still, I hang on. I must hang on because if I let go, especially with Hunter, I may break.

I suck as hard as I can, sliding my hand around the base of his length.

Hunter gives another shudder and groan, and I keep sucking. But when I try to take him deeper again, he sits up straight.

"Winter. Stop."

I keep my mouth latched to his dick, but Hunter's a professional athlete. He pulls backward in a swift motion that forces me to release my hold on his erection, and I go tumbling onto my back on the floor.

Hunter stands up and tucks his impressive package back into his jeans. He zips himself up and then drops down to the floor next to me.

Kneeling by my head, he looks directly into my eyes.

"What's going on, Princess?"

Emotion clogs my throat. "What do you mean?"

"I mean why do you not want to be touched?"

I go still.

Because...

He noticed.

Despite my efforts to suck him off and get him too turned on to think straight, Hunter noticed my pain.

Of course he did.

Hunter's always noticed everything about me.

He helps me to a sitting position and takes my chin between his thumb and forefinger. "Tell me."

I grit my teeth together and shake my head.

"Winter." His tone gentles. "Please."

When I still don't respond, he picks me up in his arms and carries me upstairs and to his bed.

CHAPTER TWELVE

Hunter puts me on his bed and plants a kiss on my forehead.

He crosses the room to his dresser and tosses me a red t-shirt from his drawer. "You can put this on," he says as he heads for his attached bathroom. "I'll give you some privacy and be right back."

With shaking hands, I peel off my jeans and top and cover myself with Hunter's soft, cotton t-shirt before I pull back his thick, green, down comforter and off-white sheets and snuggle under the covers.

When Hunter returns from the bathroom, he turns out every light except for one soft light on the nightstand by his side of the bed, and then he climbs in behind me. I don't move until I feel his arm go around me. Then, I scoot backward until my back is pressed to his front.

His hand barely touches my stomach as he murmurs in my ear, "Who hurt you, Princess?"

I let out a shaky sigh. "It's a long story, Hunt. One I haven't told anyone here about. Not my parents, not Peyton or Ashley. You'd be the first."

"Do you trust me?"

"You know I do."

"Good. Because I'm not going anywhere. You don't have to tell me tonight or tomorrow, but when you're ready, I'm here."

I know he's here. And if I'm going to heal, I need to tell Hunter the truth.

"A director on Broadway tried to rape me."

The words sound stark and cold in the warm cocoon of his bed.

Hunter's hand briefly curls into a fist, but then he slowly lets his fingers relax.

"Winter." His voice is pained. "I'm sorry."

His words are to the point, and I take his hand in mine and hold it close to me.

"It was six months ago, but I'm not over it yet. Maybe I never will be." I close my eyes, remembering how powerless I felt and how alone. "He was a powerful man in the industry, and he was at an audition session I attended. A lot of actors and actresses tried out, but I felt really good about my audition. It was just one of those moments where I felt totally at one with the character. He noticed. I saw him glance up from his notes, and afterward, he singled me out. He asked to talk to me for a moment."

Hunter's hand tightens around mine.

"I remember being so excited, thinking this was my chance to finally land a lead on my own. Seasonal Bliss was my career break, but I got my opportunity because the lead broke her ankle. I was determined to get a big role all on my own this time."

I stare down at Hunter's large hand covering my smaller one. It gives me the strength to continue.

"The director led me down the hallway and into a private office. I didn't think anything of it. I had met with my Seasonal Bliss director many times in his office without incident. Anyway, he had me take a seat across from his desk, and at first, he just asked me questions about my Broadway experience and so on. But then, he stood up and came up behind me. He put his hands on my shoulders and started playing with my hair." I bite my lip, hating the memory of his hands on me. "I stood up immediately and told him I needed to leave."

"Win..." Hunter sounds tortured.

"But he just reached behind him and flipped the lock on the door. And my heart came into my throat when I realized what I had gotten myself into."

"You didn't get yourself into anything." Hunter's voice is steel. "He broke every professional boundary."

"I know. It's just one of those moments I replay over and over—if I had just refused to enter his office..." I grit my teeth and force the next words out. "He unzipped his pants and asked me to touch him. I said no and tried to get to the door. He cornered me against the wall. And he said he'd only ask me nicely once more."

"Christ." Hunter's entire body has gone rigid.

"He pressed me up against the wall so I couldn't move. He was behind me, and he held my wrists together hard and rubbed up against me..." I stifle a pained sound. "He lifted up my skirt and forced himself between my legs, first his hand and then his..." I swallow the rest of the terrible sentence. "By the grace of God, before he could fully carry out his plan, a knock on his door made him pause. It was his assistant saying he had an important call that couldn't wait. The interruption must have made him worried that he'd be caught. He let me go, made me fix my skirt, and told me if I said anything, he'd make sure I never got another role on Broadway ever again. He swore he'd blacklist me. Then, he opened the door. I ran like hell and right into Pat, my manager, who was looking for me."

"Did you tell him?"

I twist around so I can look Hunter in the eye. His expression is taut, his jaw clenched, but his hand on my hip is gentle.

"I didn't have to say a word for him to know something was wrong. He's been around the block in the world of theater. He walked me outside and asked me what happened." I take a deep breath. "I told him the truth. He supported me in going to the police. I was sure about my decision to turn the asshole in. I told the cops my side of the story, but they said it would be my word against his, and without any witnesses, the case would most likely be a lost cause. Despite how rough he'd been with me, I had no bruising or any signs of physical abuse. They told me he'd claim it was consensual. Not only that, they said he had a lot of power in the city and taking him on and winning would be nearly impossible. I filed the report anyway, and then I went back to my apartment and tried to figure out if there was anything else I could do."

"Bastard deserves to have his dick cut off."

"I never saw him again. I hid out in my apartment and didn't go on any auditions. A week or so after I reported him, a second woman came forward. She had been attacked a year before. Then, three more women came forward. He was let go from his position as director. And that was a big deal—he's a legend in that world. He's got a lot of connections and a lot of money, so I don't know if he'll ever go to prison. His attorneys managed to delay a trial. There may be a settlement. But hopefully, with the light shining on him like this, he won't hurt anyone again."

I stop talking, and the room goes deathly quiet as Hunter softly plays with the bunched fabric of his t-shirt at my waist.

"Thank you for trusting me, Win." The anger I know he feels on my behalf is still in his voice, but he's speaking softly. "I legitimately want to take my truck up to New York City and hunt that fucker down."

I open my mouth, but before I can protest, he keeps talking. "I won't. I know that wouldn't help you. You handled an incredibly challenging situation far better than I would have."

I shift closer to him until my chest is pressed against his. "I wish that were true, Hunt. Every audition I've gone on since that one has been a disaster. It's like I'm afraid if I do well, I'll have the same experience. I know it's irrational, and that asshole isn't even working there anymore, but I can't shake it. At the last audition, I strained my vocal cords to the point the doctor told me I had to rest my voice for a few weeks. That's when Pat sent me home."

Hunter's arms circle around my back, and he hugs me close. "This is the reason you're back here? No wonder you didn't want to talk about it."

"I think Pat thought home would heal me."

"Maybe it will." Hunter sounds a hell of a lot surer than I am.

But as I drift off to sleep in his arms, I wonder if he can help me.

"I want to ask you a question," I say, already half-asleep.

"Tomorrow, darling." Hunter's hand rubs my back. "Go to sleep, and we'll talk tomorrow."

CHAPTER THIRTEEN

I wake up in the morning to the feeling of being wrapped in a very warm blanket. The blanket is super heavy, and as I try to move, it wraps around me more tightly.

"Where are you going?" The voice is raspy and low.

I bite down on a gasp as I remember last night.

Hunter.

Me taking him in my mouth.

Me freaking out.

Him bringing me to his bed.

Where I still am.

And where his warm body is currently spooning me from behind.

Crap, this is going to be awkward.

I turn around in his arms.

His green eyes are open, and he's looking at me carefully. Like he's afraid I may break like a piece of china.

"How are you feeling?" he asks me.

"I'm fine," I say quickly. "Honestly. I kind of wish last night could be erased from existence, though—like a number of nights from our past."

My attempt at a joke works, and Hunter's expression relaxes into a grin.

"Darling, I don't think you want to erase our nights together. We've got some good moments in there, right?"

I reach up and tousle his hair, which is messy from sleep. "We do. Sexy moments interspersed with either fighting or confessions or pain..."

He silences me by putting a finger over my lips. "Hey." His tone turns serious. "I wouldn't take last night back for anything. I hate that you went through that, though. *That* I would give anything to take back."

I swallow. "I'll be okay."

"I know you will. Doesn't mean any of it feels fair."

A distinct purring sound distracts us, and we both look down to find Theo at our feet. When he sees us notice him, he stands up and meows loudly.

"Theo, are you hungry?" I reach over and pet him affectionately. "I'll feed you, honey."

But Hunter holds me in place. "I'll do it. You stay in and rest. It's still early."

"You must be exhausted after your game last night."

"I'm okay. Plus, I have to meet my brothers for breakfast before they fly back to Montana." As if on cue, his phone buzzes on the nightstand.

I admire how the muscles ripple across his back as he sits up. When he turns back to face me, my gaze wanders down his bare chest, and without meaning to, I reach out and run my hand down his abs.

"So I was thinking," I begin.

But he just shakes his head and kisses my forehead. "Later," he says in a rough tone. "Okay?"

"Sure. Later."

He pauses. "Liam asked me to babysit tonight. We don't have a game, and he and Cathy need a night alone. Do you want to come with me?"

I freeze. "To babysit your niece? I've never met her before."

"So consider this your first meeting." His eyes lock with mine. "What do you say?"

This feels like a date.

And Hunter and I don't date. At least, we've never really tried to date. Because I think we both know how disastrous that could be.

But I want to see him with his niece, and I want to spend time with him far too much to turn him down.

So I answer with, "I say yes."

———

Hunter

"What the hell was that kiss?" Jared asks me the moment I meet him, Max, and Liam at Café du Monde.

The four of us are interrupted by a slew of autograph and selfie seekers, and by the time we finally snag a private table in the back, I was sure everyone would forget Jared's question.

No such luck.

Liam grins. "That's Hunt's *I-don't-like-my-housemate-can't-you-tell* kiss."

I shoot him a dirty look. "Asshole."

Jared and Max exchange looks. "She's not distracting you from hockey, is she?" Jared asks me.

"Like Ashley can distract you?" I counter.

His lip curls in annoyance. "Leave Ashley out of this."

"Why?" Liam says, his brow cocked. "Did you two..."

"Nothing. We were nothing," Jared says quickly. "Friends. That's it."

Liam and I exchange a look while Max assesses Jared curiously.

"Was she the girl in high school who you said you..." Max doesn't get a chance to finish his sentence.

"I said to shut it about Ashley." The hardness in Jared's voice is unmistakable, and whenever he sounds like that, we all know to back off.

Liam quickly changes the subject, and the four of us chat about hockey. Of course, they make sure to give me shit about my slump, but I have the last word given my game last night, and they all know it.

"You could still win MVP," Max says to me. "You've got the line for it, and if you keep playing like you did last night, it's yours to take."

"We'll see," is all I say. "I'm pretty sure your all-world captain's got it locked up."

"Who, Wild?" Max shrugs. "Declan Wild's already won it three times in his career. Besides, everybody around the league knows that—despite your recent little wobble—" He flashes me a grin—"your play this season is a big reason why New Orleans has a shot to make something happen in the playoffs. And the league loves to give it to somebody new. That could be you, man."

"Back to the previous topic," Liam says to me. "The one that's the name of this glorious season we're currently in."

"Jesus, Liam." I glare at him. "Give it a rest, will you?"

But our oldest brother never did learn to keep his mouth shut. "What do you expect us to think? You and Winter Allen have always been combustible."

"I know that," I say curtly.

"And if you fuck her," he says in a tone that edges on concern, "It will end badly."

I roll my shoulders and wait until we've all ordered our beignets and café au laits before I speak. "It's different now," I say.

"How?" Jared asks curiously.

"It just...it is." I choose my words carefully, but I can't keep the emotion out of them.

Last night with Winter pushed every single one of my buttons. The way her mouth felt on mine, and then when she wrapped her lips around my dick—I nearly came right down her throat.

But that would have been the wrong thing to do. Winter wasn't acting like herself. And I could tell. Despite how little blood flow was in my head, I knew she was acting differently. Off. And it was a sucker punch to the gut when I found out the truth. If I could destroy that fucker who assaulted her, I wouldn't hesitate for a second.

"What do you mean?" Liam presses me.

I suck in a breath. "You're testing the absolute limits of my patience. Back the fuck off."

"What's up with you and Cath, Liam?" Jared pipes in. "She seemed pretty pissed last night when we got back to your place."

"Save it." Liam's eyes turn to stone. "She's tired. You try taking care of a kid all day long."

"Hey, I wasn't criticizing Cath," Jared says as he, Max, and I exchange a glance. "I just meant—are you two okay?"

"Fine." Liam nods thank you to the waiter as he delivers our drinks and beignets.

And then, we all shut up so we can eat. That, and to potentially avoid a fistfight.

The four of us love each other, no doubt. We'd have each other's backs in a knife fight without question. But we don't communicate all that well. Okay, our communication skills are pretty much shit.

Not having a mother around since we were kids probably didn't help us in the emotional expression department. Not that all dads are closed off, but ours was. Mama was the nurturer. She wanted to know about your day and if anything was going on that you wanted to share. Dad was the most supportive father a kid could ask for, but his idea of a heart-to-heart was to grunt, hand you a deck of cards, and tell you to start shuffling because we were about to play a game of poker.

My brothers and I stuff our faces and chat a bit more about the season, and then we all stand up and head for the sidewalk.

Max and Jared need to go to the airport, and the Storm brothers are about to split up once more. None of us act like we'll miss each other, but we're all lying.

The truth is that it's hard playing on opposing teams. And it's even harder living so far apart. The four of us have been tight our whole lives, and after Dad was killed, we just got closer.

We around the corner of the building hoping for some privacy, but a few fans manage to find us anyway.

I take a photo with an appreciative couple, and when I turn around, Max is being hounded by a zealous blonde who wants him to sign her hat. He does so with a quick grin, but when she goes to hug him, he steps backward so she can't touch him.

"Typical Max," Liam mutters to me as Jared diverts the blonde's attention by offering to take a photo with her.

Max is definitely the most introverted of the four of us. Unlike some of the players I know who crave the attention, especially from their female fans, Max prefers to go under cover as much as humanly possible.

The fans drift away, and the four of us are alone again. Liam and I say our goodbyes to the twins with a couple of hugs and back slaps.

"Hold up." Liam reaches out to stop Jared from hailing a cab. "I may have news soon. The detective contacted me last week."

"He did?" I spin on him. "Why the fuck didn't you tell anyone?"

"Telling you now," is all he says, and Jared curses.

"He's considering reopening the case."

The three of us stare at Liam.

"Why?" I say. "That must mean..."

"He said there may be new evidence. And they have a couple of suspects." Liam's voice is so low I have to strain to hear him. "We may need to look at another lineup."

I clench my hand into a fist. "Those lineups haven't done us any good so far."

"I still think we're going to find him," Max says, his eyes haunted. "I've always thought that. Maybe this is the time." Maybe. Or maybe we're going down another dead end.

———

Practice feels like another game. Between Liam's news and what happened with Winter last night, I'm amped.

I score on a breakaway, flicking the puck into the net like the goalie's not even there. Wyatt's a great goalie—he's been an all-star the last three years, and he rips off his mask and stares at me. I reach past him to grab the puck, trying not to make eye contact.

But he punches my shoulder. "Hey. Storm. Everything all right?"

I toss the puck toward center ice. "Yeah. Fine."

Wyatt's nearly-black eyes assess me. "A woman, huh?"

I give a short laugh. "Among other things."

"Huh." He looks at me a moment longer before pulling his mask over his face. "Next time, don't go for my head. I get enough of that in real games."

"You two done screwing around?" Liam shouts from the midline. "Let's go!"

I nod at Wyatt. "Sorry, man."

I take his warning to heart and dial back my aggressiveness for the rest of practice. But, that doesn't stop me from scoring another two goals. Today was supposed to be a light scrimmage, and eventually, Coach tells me to sit on the bench.

"Save it," he snaps. "You looked good out there last night, Storm. We've got a road trip coming up this week. I don't want you leaving this newfound energy on the practice ice."

I won't. But as soon as practice is over, thoughts of Winter pervade my mind.

When I'm showering and changing in the locker room.

When I decline Murph and Dean's invitation to grab dinner. When I hop into my truck and pull out of the parking lot.

And as I walk up the front steps of my house and see Winter napping on the porch with Theo on her lap, my heart feels far more involved than I'm comfortable with.

Winter and I can't be anything more than friends. We can't.

That's what I tell myself as I drop my bag quietly on the floor.

She opens her eyes. "Hi, Hunt."

"Hey." I bend over and brush a stray hair off of her cheek.

"How was practice? And your brothers?" She sits up and adds with a smile, "They bugged you about us, didn't they?"

"Of course they did," I say. "But don't worry. I shut them up and told them nothing."

"Thank you."

We stare at each other for a beat.

"Look..." she says.

"Do you..." I start.

We both laugh, and I shake my head. "You go first."

"Actually, I have something to ask you," she says.

"Shoot." I take a seat on the porch swing with Theo between us.

He's happy as can be, purring loudly while Winter pets him.

"I have a proposition for you," she says.

"Okay." I cross my ankle over the opposite knee and shift to face her fully.

"I want to heal while I'm home. Completely heal."

"Right. I agree. You deserve that."

She nods. "So...one way I need to heal is physically." She pauses. "Sexually."

I stare at her. "Okay. I'm not sure..."

"Will you help me?" she says so fast those four words almost sound like one.

I freeze. "Help you how?"

"Help me to enjoy sex again." Her cheeks go pink as she

keeps her eyes fastened to mine. "To feel safe being with some-one. To be touched. Everywhere."

And...my dick twitches.

But I keep my expression blank. "You haven't been with anyone since..."

She shakes her head. "I've felt completely asexual since it happened. Until I saw you."

I reach for her hand. "Princess, you're going to need to spell this out for me—what exactly do you want me to do?"

"I want you to fuck me."

CHAPTER FOURTEEN

The air on the porch just got a hell of a lot thicker.

I tug at the neck of my sweatshirt like I can somehow cool myself off.

"Do you want to date? Because I—" *Suck at that. Can't imagine doing that with you and then watching you leave for New York in six months*—"I don't normally do that."

"No. I just want to have sex. No strings attached, hot, sweaty sex. As much as possible."

Jesus Christ. She's going to kill me.

I run my thumb over her soft palm. "I'll do anything for you, Winter. But this? This is a big deal. I don't know that we can do what you're asking and not get in too deep."

"Because…"

"Because it's us, Win. We're two people with history. A lot of history. And we've never tried a friends-with-benefits arrangement before. Is that what this would be?"

"I guess so." Her face flashes with vulnerability, and for the first time, she looks totally unsure. "I'm not really sure what it would be. I just know that you're literally the only man on the planet I can imagine getting naked with right now. And that has to mean something, right?"

Right. I don't want to dip too far into what exactly that could mean.

So, I stand up.

"Let's get ready to go to Liam's for our night with Lulu," I say. "If you still feel the same way later, we'll talk some more."

"Are you—"

I know where she's going with this, and I cut her off at the pass. "Not turning you down." I lean down and give her a firm kiss on the lips. "I just want you to be sure, Win. Because once we..." I lock eyes with her. Her blue eyes are swimming with emotion. "Once we take that step, it will change everything between us. Even if it's just sex."

Just sex.

I nearly scoff at the very concept. I already know without a shadow of a doubt that sex with Winter is going to alter my universe. Permanently.

———

Winter

Liam greets Hunter and me at his front door. "A two for one babysitting deal, huh?" he jokes as he kisses me on the cheek.

"I used to babysit as a teenager," I say. "I doubt I remember anything though. Being an only child didn't give me a lot of experience with little kids."

Cathy's in the living room with Lulu in her arms. "You'll be fine," she says to me as I hug her hello. "I don't know what I'm doing half the time either."

"She's adorable." I smile at Lulu, who tries to lunge out of her mama's arms toward Hunter behind me.

"She does that every time Hunter comes over," Cathy says with a laugh.

Hunter appeases his niece by taking her into his arms and kissing her cheek. She squeals with delight.

And my heart damn near melts in a puddle right on the floor.

Because Hunter's guard just drops around Lulu. He's so relaxed, so...happy. His expression is open and filled with love as he snuggles Lulu into his chest.

Cathy leads me into the kitchen and shows me where everything is. As she's pointing out where the plates and utensils are, I notice Liam and Hunter in deep conversation in the living room.

Hunter's eyes flash with anger, and Liam puts his hand on Hunt's shoulder like he's urging him to calm down.

Cathy finishes her tour, she and Liam say goodbye, and they're gone.

It's just Hunter, me, and a baby.

I'm happy for the distraction after the way I made a fool of myself earlier when I propositioned him—*literally*. My cheeks burn at the memory, and I force those thoughts out of my mind and smile as Hunter swings Lulu into the air, making sure to never let her go.

"I'm starved," he says to me. "Are you?"

"Sure. But you know how good I am at cooking. Shall we order a pizza?" I ask.

He glances over at me. "Like old times."

I smile. "You remember."

"Of course I remember. It was our first kiss."

"Yes." I smile back at him. "It was."

We were at a classmate's party, and everyone was drinking. Hunter and I were the only ones who admitted to being hungry, and we were desperately craving a pizza.

All the restaurants we tried were already closed for the night or didn't deliver. Finally, we lucked out with the last place we called.

We smuggled that pizza like a secret treasure into an empty bedroom where we sat on the floor and devoured every slice. And yes, we kissed. A lot.

Over Lulu's head, Hunter's eyes fix on my mouth.

I'm so turned on I have to avert my gaze. "I'll get my phone."

An hour and a half later, the pizza box sitting between us on the living room couch is empty, and Lulu is sound asleep on Hunter's chest. I reach for the remote.

"You want to watch a movie?"

"Sure. You pick."

I laugh. "Right. Let's see how long that attitude lasts."

Hunter smirks. "It's not my fault your taste in movies sucks."

"*My* taste? I seem to remember you have a penchant for horror flicks."

"I do. I'm a guy. We like that shit. And you girls like chick flicks."

"Oh my God—you're so stereotypical. Not all females like Ryan Gosling movies. I, for one, am not a fan."

"What do you like then? I'm not sure I ever figured it out."

His statement hangs heavy between us, and I flick my gaze to his. "I'm pretty sure you did, Hunt. More than once."

He moves the pizza box to the coffee table and, with Lulu still sleeping on his chest, he shifts closer to me so that our thighs are touching.

I can smell his aftershave, and the minty scent is so heady my lower belly clenches. I'm so attracted to this man it's ridiculous. I take a moment to thank God that at least my body's not permanently broken.

"I'm starting to think you're the main reason I came home," I murmur.

"Because I can get you off?" His words are a whisper in my ear.

"That hasn't been proven yet." I press the remote's "on" button and start flipping through the options. "You haven't accepted my offer."

"That's true. I haven't." His free hand snakes over to my thigh. "But I'm pretty sure I will."

"You...are?" My voice comes out so hoarse I'm not sure he

understood what I just said. I'm flipping through the channels without even seeing what's on, but I can't stop because I don't know what the hell else to do with my hands.

"When have I ever turned you down?" His tone is serious.

I swallow. "Let's focus on picking a movie for now. We have little ears in the room with us."

"Sleeping ears." His hand drags slowly up my thigh, and I let out a small moan. "I vote on that movie right there."

I refocus my glazed eyes. Hunter's choice is a feel-good romance set in the winter backdrop of the Colorado mountains.

"Why this movie?" I ask him. "So not your style."

"True. But I'm in the mood for a happy ending tonight."

As the movie starts playing, I sneak a peek at him. "Is everything okay?" I ask him. "You and Liam seemed to be having a tense moment earlier."

Definitely a tense moment. At the very mention of it, Hunter's jaw tightens.

"It's not my business, of course," I say. "I didn't mean to put you on the spot."

"You didn't." He gives my leg a quick squeeze. "I'll tell you about it when we're back home."

"Okay." I look at him a moment longer, and then we settle in to watch the movie.

Like Hunter, I'm in the mood for a happily ever after, and this film fits the bill perfectly.

By the time Liam and Cathy return, Hunter and I have put Lulu to bed, cleaned up from dinner, and are nearly asleep on the couch.

"You two look like an old married couple," Liam comments as Cathy goes to check on Lulu.

I stand up and grab my coat. "Your teasing hasn't eased up since you got older," I say to him.

"Hey, it's called being the oldest." He grins, his smile so similar to Hunter's and his green eyes flashing with mischief.

All the Storm boys are hot as hell, but I've always only had eyes for one.

I pat Liam goodbye on the arm. "Thanks for introducing me to your daughter."

"Thanks for coming over." He shoots a look at Hunter over my head. "Maybe you'll stay in town permanently, huh?"

I fidget with the zipper on my coat. "Last I checked, Broadway's zip code wasn't in New Orleans. You know Broadway—where my career is?"

"Last I checked, you didn't need Broadway to be a success."

When I gawk at him, Liam just winks at me and then walks us out.

CHAPTER FIFTEEN

Hunter and I drive home in a comfortable silence broken when I ask if he's exhausted from his game yesterday.

"I slept well last night, that's for sure," he says.

I flush, remembering his arms around me when I woke up this morning.

Like he's reading my mind, he adds, "I liked having my arms around you, Winter."

"Me, too."

"It sure beats living with Murph in a hotel room."

I laugh. "Are you two always roommates?"

"Not always. We don't get a choice in the matter, but Coach often puts me with Murph. He tries to pair guys who won't kill each other by morning. Speaking of, I've got a ten-day road trip starting tomorrow."

"That's right." I'd completely forgotten it was coming up so soon. "I saw your schedule on the fridge."

"Will you miss me?" he asks.

I know he's half-kidding, but I decide to answer him anyway. "Yes, I'll miss you."

We're pulling into his driveway, and as we exit the truck, he says to me, "My house is yours, Win. Be sure to make yourself at home while I'm away."

We walk through the porch and into the living room. As Hunter switches off the alarm, Theo comes down off his cat tower to greet us with a stretch and a meow.

Hunter goes to scoop his litter box while I put out a can of cat food for him.

Theo's happily eating when Hunter returns to the living room with a sealed bag in his hand from the litter box.

"I'm going to dispose of this," he says as he steps outside.

I follow him with the filled recycling box, and I dump it into the recycling bin while he tosses the poop bag into the garbage.

He shoves his hands in his pockets. "Bet you don't hear quiet like this in Manhattan."

I smile. "You sound like your brother. Trying to get me to stay here."

"Who, me?" He puts his arm around me as we climb the steps together and re-enter the house. "I was just surmising."

"Huh." I take a seat on the living room couch. "New York is where Broadway is. And Broadway's my place. Just like hockey's yours."

His eyes burn into mine. "I get it. I would never try to take you away from your thing, Win. I'm happy for you."

While I'm putting on a good show, the truth is that I'm not sure Broadway is my *thing*. Not anymore. But I don't have a clue how to start over or what that would look like, and I'm not ready to share my feelings with anyone yet.

I pull my gaze away from his and say in a teasing tone, "You and Liam wouldn't understand New York City, anyway."

Hunter lifts up Theo and sits on the couch with him on his lap. He's across from me, but I stretch my legs out on the couch so they're nearly touching his.

"You say that like neither of us have ever been there," he says with a grin. "We're going there tomorrow for a game, darling."

"I know you've been to New York." *Crap*. I didn't mean to say that.

"Because you've followed my games." His tone is curious.

"Yes. And because...I thought of reaching out a time or two in the past ten years. So, when I knew you were in town, I thought of it more."

"Winter, every time we went to New York to play, I thought of you. But you and I...we promised to make a clean break when you left. And I didn't want to jeopardize the great things you were doing on your own." A shadow crosses his face. "I fucking hate that I didn't reach out. If I'd known you were suffering, you know I would have been there for you."

"I know."

"Do you?"

I nod. "Life just kind of marched on the last six months. Really, it marched on the last decade, and before I knew it, ten years had passed. But I'm here now."

"You are." His hand that's petting Theo stills. "I'm glad you're here, Princess."

"Me, too. Seeing you and your brothers again has been nice. You've obviously built something special for yourselves. You've turned your whole lives around. After your dad..." I choke up. "I'm sorry."

Hunter's big hand grasps my ankle that's closest to him. "Liam said they're thinking about re-examining the case."

His green eyes are fathomlessly deep, and the pain that just came to the surface slays me.

"Oh my gosh. Hunt." I wince. "Do you know why?"

"They have new evidence, apparently. We may need to look at a line-up again."

I can't imagine what it would be like, as a teenager, asked to identify my father's possible killer. I can't imagine doing it as an adult either.

"I'm so sorry. If you need to do that, I'll go with you."

His head jerks slightly. Just enough that I notice.

He doesn't want to let me in. Not like that. I try not to let on how much that stings.

Hunter's always been a close-to-the-vest kind of guy. He was torn up after Mrs. Storm died when all four boys were young. When his dad was murdered, another piece of Hunt's heart shuttered, and I don't know that he'll ever open it fully again.

"If you want support," I add quickly. "I won't crowd you."

His lips twitch. "Princess, you're the opposite of a cager."

Maybe so. Maybe I always was more interested in things other than an intimate relationship.

But tonight, what I'm most interested in is sitting across from me tenderly holding onto my ankle.

"So. Not to change the subject or anything..."

"Please." His eyes plead with me. "Please change the subject."

"To get back to what we discussed earlier today—my answer is still the same," I say. "If you're willing to help me, that is."

Hunter's eyes darken. "You're aware of the risks."

"Yes."

He picks up Theo and puts him directly on the couch cushion. Then, he leans closer and cups my cheek tenderly. "I'm honored you trust me enough. I'll do my best to anticipate what you need, but I may need some guidance from you along the way. I'm sure, actually, that I'll need guidance."

I nod. "Okay."

He takes my hand in his. "You want to start tonight?"

Another nod from me. "Yes."

He stands up, tugs me behind him, and heads for his bedroom, flicking off the lights in the living room and hall as we go.

Once we're in his room, he urges me onto his bed, and then he crawls up next to me. Propping his head up on his hand with his elbow on the mattress, he says, "Let's talk first."

"That's a good idea."

"I'm game for anything—and everything—that you are." His

gaze is molten with heat. "But I do want this to be exclusive. I know it will have an expiration date and that when you return to your real life, what's between us will end."

My real life.

I'm not sure I know what's real and what's not anymore.

"But while you're here and we're doing this, I don't want anyone else in either of our beds."

I sigh. "Obviously, with my issue, I won't…"

"I mean once you heal," he clarifies. "Because you will heal, Winter."

"But once I heal…"

"You think we'll stop?" He runs a finger down my cheek. "If that's what you want, we will. But I already know I'll want as much as you'll give me, darling."

A full-body shiver goes through me at his words. "Okay. Exclusive. But how do you know I'll heal?"

"Because when have you ever not gotten something you set your mind to?"

I shrug. "This is my body, not my mind. I can't just mind-over-matter it."

Hunter reaches for my waist and, hooking his thumb into my belt loop, he tugs me up against him. "No, but you can trust again." His mouth lands on mine, and my thighs clench. His kiss is firm and certain.

My hands go to the hem of his t-shirt, and I slide my hands underneath to his hot skin. I run my fingers over his ribs and up to his defined chest. Meanwhile, his tongue slides inside my mouth, and emotion unexpectedly fills my throat.

Hunter's right. I *can* trust again. Because I'm with him.

The realization breaks the dam inside of me.

For six months, I never cried about what happened. Not one time.

But right now, tears fall down my cheeks as Hunter kisses me. When he hesitates, I beg him to keep going.

"Are you sure?" His voice is uncertain.

"I've never been more sure of anything. This is exactly what I need," I promise him. "You are exactly what I need, Hunter. Please don't let me down."

His teeth sink gently into my neck as he unhooks my bra. When his thumb brushes over my bare breast, my hips start bucking against him.

"Take off my clothes," I say into his mouth. "I want you to rock my world."

He groans as his tongue tangles with mine. "Win, you're the one who's gonna rock mine."

By the time we're both naked, I'm still emotional, but now I'm moaning. Hunter reaches off the bed and into his jeans pocket. When he leans over me with a condom in his hand, I shake my head vigorously.

"No. No condom," I say to him. "I can't."

"But..." Confusion flashes over his face.

"He...when he..." I choke on the words. "He whipped out a condom, and so it reminds me..."

Hunter tosses the condom into the trash immediately. "I'll pull out," he promises me.

But I shake my head. "I'm on the pill. You don't have to pull out. It's all good as long as you're clean. I am. I was checked after that...and I haven't been with anyone since."

"I was checked right before you came home, and I haven't even looked at another woman since I opened my door to you." His mouth closes over mine. "I never look at anyone else when you're in my life, Princess."

As he positions himself over me, he freezes. "I'm sorry. You should be on top."

"Why?"

"Because this probably reminds you...makes you feel trapped or scared."

I shake my head again. "He didn't...this wasn't the position we were in when he tried to...he was behind me."

Hunter runs a hand over his face. "Right. You said that...

okay." He kisses me again. "This is harder than I thought it would be, Winter. I don't want to talk about what happened to you while we're in bed together, but it keeps coming up, and I feel like that's my fault. I just want you to know you're safe."

"I do." I look at him. "We've waited a long time for this."

His green eyes are liquid with emotion. "I've wanted to do this with you since we were teenagers."

"Me, too."

But a lot changed in ten years, and I tense as Hunter shifts to go inside me.

He pushes slowly—so slowly—but I'm braced for discomfort. The attack hurt so much physically and emotionally. I thought I'd never get over the trauma of when that prick tried to force his way inside me without my permission. Even though I got away, the damage was done, and I never wanted anyone that close to me again. I haven't even put my own fingers inside myself since.

But as Hunter slowly enters me, stretching and filling the most vulnerable part of my body, I feel good.

"You okay?" He goes still inside me.

"Yes. I'm good."

"Relax and breathe." His voice is in my ear. "It will help with any tension. Breathe for me, Win."

I let out a deep breath, and he slides in even more. And, oh God, I want him deeper.

"More," I say, my voice sounding husky. "I need you deeper."

He pushes further in and then stops moving. Our eyes lock. Holy shit, I'm so crazy for him I can hardly stop from saying how I feel out loud.

"Hunter."

The emotion on his face overwhelms me. "I know." He puts his cheek to mine. "I feel it, too. I knew I'd feel it. You're going to shatter me for anyone else ever again."

He drives inside me more deeply and then drags himself out. And then, he does it again.

By the third time, I'm begging him, "Faster. Please."

He obliges.

"Harder, Hunt."

His thrusts become longer and deeper. The more he moves, the more I meet his thrusts halfway, my hips bucking off the bed to keep up.

"So good, Princess. Fuck, do you know how much you turn me on? Do you know how good it feels to have my cock inside your sweet heat?"

Hunter's dirty talk spurs me on, and I feel myself clenching around him. He curses into my neck and keeps murmuring into my ear.

He talks to me the entire time, telling me how perfect I feel, how turned on he is, and how incredibly hard he's going to come. But not until I do, he whispers. If it takes the rest of my time in New Orleans, he's not going to come until I do.

Well, he won't have to wait long. My orgasm starts small, so tiny that I hardly recognize it, but then it builds, and by the time I'm in full crescendo, the waves of pleasure are so big I'm saying Hunter's name over and over like a chant.

He follows me into release, calling out, "Win" as he thrusts hard into me and then collapses with his face buried in my shoulder.

We stay still for over a minute, catching our breath and coming down from the high.

"We're definitely doing that again," I say.

He lifts his head and looks into my eyes. His have a wicked gleam to them. "Damn straight we are."

CHAPTER SIXTEEN

Hunter

For the second morning in a row, I wake up with my arm wrapped around Winter's warm body.

But unlike yesterday morning, today things are clear between us. As clear as either of us are willing to make them.

I drag my hand down Winter's smooth skin until I reach her thigh. I turn her just enough that she rolls onto her back as she lets out a little sigh in her sleep, and then I whisper in her ear, "Do you want to be touched?"

She opens her eyes.

I lean in and kiss her bare shoulder. "I would love to have woken you up with my head between your legs..."

She lets out a moan.

"But I didn't want to take you by surprise like that."

After what she told me about being attacked, I want to make sure I always get clear consent from Winter before I do anything intimate.

"I appreciate that, Hunt." She ruffles my hair. "I don't think I'm ready to be surprised yet. But someday..."

Yes, someday Winter will fully heal. Hopefully soon. But definitely before she leaves town, when she'll head back to New

York. And at that point...maybe she'll meet someone new. My chest lurches at the very idea, and I force the thought out of my head.

She's watching my face carefully. "Something wrong?" she asks me with concern.

"No." I say it quickly.

She takes my hand in hers and moves them both down her bare body and between her legs.

"I'd like you to touch me," she says.

"With my fingers?" I ask her.

"And your..." She catches her breath.

"My...my what?" I love the way she squirms when she's turned on. I can feel her getting wet where our hands are joined between her legs.

"Your tongue."

"You want my tongue on you?"

She bites her lip before releasing it to say, "Yes. A lot."

"A lot of my tongue?"

She reveals that genuine Winter smile I love so much. "A lot of your tongue, and I want that a lot. A lot, a lot."

I ghost her mouth with mine. "Okay," I whisper.

I slide down her body until my face is between her legs. I stroke one finger inside her folds and she arches to meet my tongue.

I feel two hands grip my head. "Oh God, Hunt. Don't stop."

I don't. She tastes like a dewy morning in New Orleans—hot and sweet, and the taste drugs me. I'm so hard I honest to God could come without being touched.

"So good." She bucks up into my face.

I couldn't agree more.

I taste every ounce of Winter's arousal, and I keep going, determined to tip her over the edge into bliss.

I've only kissed Winter like this once before, and we were just a couple weeks away from her moving to New York City. But

I memorized the moment, and I learned what she liked and how she liked it.

I slip two fingers inside her as I kiss her most sensitive spot.

"Hunt..."

She draws out my name, the southern accent she's worked so hard to destroy coming back strong. I smile into her wet heat and keep kissing her until I feel her spasm around my fingers.

She calls out my name as she comes, and I keep my mouth on her throughout her orgasm.

When I feel her fully relax, I crawl up her body and lie next to her, my head sharing her pillow.

"Good morning."

She turns her head to face me. "Do you plan to wake me up that way again sometime? Because I wouldn't complain at all."

Neither would I.

———

I don't want to go on this road trip.

I never enjoy staying in hotels and flying back and forth at all hours of the night from one city to another. But that's not why I'm decidedly against this particular trip.

No, I'm actually looking forward to the games. Now that I'm coming out of my slump, I've been enjoying hockey again.

What I'm dreading is leaving Winter for ten days.

She kisses me goodbye in the kitchen and jokes that this is why I hired her—so I'd have someone to pet sit Theo without having to worry about kenneling him or scheduling someone to come over. But her eyes tell a different story. She's going to miss me, too.

"I'll text you." I give her one last kiss before turning for the door. "Have a good week."

"You too. Kick some ass in your games. The girls and I are going to have a house party when you play New York." She pumps a cute, little fist in the air. "Go, Fire!"

I wink. "See you soon."

———

The plane ride to NYC is less than three hours, but that's plenty of time for an entire team of hockey players to let loose. Our coaching staff sits up at the front of the private plane and goes over game plans, and we players fill up the rest of the plane. Our owner is a young billionaire named Noah Watts, and he's pulled out all the stops to make sure New Orleans's new hockey team is well taken care of.

From the brand-new arena with trendy retail stores built around the venue to the private plane that Noah supposedly bought on his own dime, our team is a lucky group. Having our own plane is a luxury I didn't experience with my last team, and traveling on road trips with a chartered plane was always hit or miss. In New Orleans, we've got the same plane for every trip, and the seats and amenities provide ridiculous comfort, not to mention a smooth ride.

But today, I'm not thinking about much other than what it will be like to return home to Winter.

Return home to Winter.

That phrase has a nice ring to it, but I know I can't get used to what we're doing. I've never been able to hold down a relationship, and Winter's made it clear her heart is still on Broadway.

"Hey, Hunt." Dean beckons to me from where he, Wyatt, and Murph are seated around a table with Lincoln Pitt, our rookie right winger.

Lincoln's a keep-to-himself kind of guy, which I appreciate. He nods at me silently and then goes back to shuffling the deck of cards in his hands.

"We're playing poker." Murph tips his chin at me. "Want in?"

I sink down into a seat across from them.

"So." Murph waits until I've been dealt a hand before starting in with, "You and your housemate."

"I already told you and Liam and everyone else in town to fuck off," I tell him. "If you so much as say one word about Winter, I'll..."

"Hey, calm down, Hunt." Murph signals that he'll hold on his hand, and then he turns to me. "I love Winter. We grew up together, too, remember? I just want to make sure she's not too much of a distraction for you."

"You're just being a nosy fucker like always," I tell him.

He grins. "Maybe. So how's it going between you two?"

I call and toss my cards on the table. "Winter and I are just catching up. It's casual."

What's going on between Winter and me is far from casual, but my off-handed remark manages to shut Murph up for the rest of the flight.

And when we land, I can't stop myself from texting her.

Thx for letting me know you arrived safe, she writes back.

How are you and Theo?

Warmer than you probably are in the northeast. I don't miss February in NYC.

You want me to pick you up anything while I'm here? Something you miss?

I don't think you can fit a Broadway stage in your travel bag, she jokes.

You must miss it a lot. Somehow, being apart like this, I feel like she'll be more open with me.

I wait as the white dots flash while she types.

When her answer comes through, it surprises me.

I don't miss a lot of it, tbh.

To be honest. She's really serious about this.

Before I can think of a response, another text comes through.

I miss the singing. And the scripts. I always wanted to write my own script, though, rather than play a character someone else created.

Maybe you should do that while you're home. Write your own.

Maybe I should.

And you know you can sing in the Big Easy.

I guess. Oliver's made it work for him, right?

Her comment gets me thinking. I wonder if I can help out somehow. Because the bottom line is that I want Winter to be happy. If that means Broadway, then I'll support her. But her eyes were so vacant when she first showed up on my doorstep. She's only been in town a short while, and she already looks happier and healthier than she did.

I'm fucking grinning like a sap at my phone when Liam takes the seat next to me on the team bus. I look over at him. His expression is grim.

And, immediately, I guess why.

He confirms my suspicion when he says, "We have to look at a lineup as soon as we get home. They have a person of interest."

I swallow. "Wow. Here we go again."

———

I'm fired up for our game.

I'm too fired up.

I have so much damn energy pumping through my veins, and I just want to unleash my wrath on the ice.

Liam's clearly on the same page. His jaw is stone, his eyes are daggers, and he's ready to kick some ass.

As soon as the puck is dropped, he and I are of one mind.

Suffocate the opponent.

Own the puck.

Score early and often.

And we do. We're up three to nothing at the end of the first period.

In the second, I get sent to the penalty box for fighting. I'm pissed because the guy was asking for it, but I normally know better. He's New York's enforcer, and he instigates as much as he actually scores.

I sit inside the penalty box, angrily waiting for my chance to get back out there.

As soon as the buzzer sounds, I pound my blades across the ice. I don't even stop to slow down before I hurl my body into the crowd of three players fighting for the puck.

I emerge from the tangle of limbs as the victor. Turning toward the goal, I skate with the puck as hard as I can, holding off the last defenseman until only the goalie is between me and the net. I pull back my stick and let fly.

The goalie scrambles to block my shot, but the puck skims past him.

"Score by Storm!" the announcer calls out over the loud-speaker.

We pummel New York six to one. I score three goals and assist on another.

"Fuck, yeah!" Murph pounds my back as we leave the ice. "We're in first place!"

"You're back, Hunt!" Coach Jones grips my shoulder enthusi-astically. "Whatever you're doing, keep going!"

My body is going to fucking hurt tonight. But it was worth it. I'm on fire again.

The joy over our win doesn't take away from what's going on off the ice, though.

"I should be happy," Liam tells me as we head into the locker room together. "And I fucking am. But I'm also numb."

"Same," I say back as we head for the showers.

Because all the goals in the world won't bring our father back.

As the hot water runs over my aching muscles and sore as fuck shoulder where I got slammed into the boards twice tonight, the memory that I've pushed away for years returns unbidden.

The night my father was murdered, all four of us brothers were away at a hockey game. Liam was eighteen and a senior in high school, Jared and Max seventeen, and I was fifteen.

This being New Orleans, we had to travel quite a bit at the time just to find ice.

Dad came to watch us often. But not this time. This time, he had to work.

He was working the graveyard shift at the convenience store he'd been managing for years. We often stopped by to say hi to him when we drove home from a practice or a game.

That night, I remember we won our game handily. All four of us were pumped as we drove back to New Orleans, and we couldn't wait to tell Dad. He lived for our hockey games. And he worked double shifts to be able to send us out of state where we could practice our skills, compete against the top players in the country, and learn from the best.

We pulled up to the convenience store. An ambulance and three cop cars, lights flashing, were in the parking lot.

My gut turned over, and I knew something was wrong.

Before Liam had even fully stopped the car, I had the back door open and was jumping out.

Liam, Jared, and Max were right behind me.

As we ran toward the building, a guy, dressed all in black and wearing a wool hat, came out of the shadows.

All four of us looked right at him.

He was of average height and build. The only distinct feature I noticed was a clear, brownish-red mark on his right cheek.

As I went to look at him more closely, he averted his gaze before I could see his eyes.

Something about him wasn't right. He was jittery and seemed high. And that bulge in his jacket pocket—was that a weapon?

He pushed past us and ran into the woods behind the convenience store.

"What the—" Jared made a move to chase after him, but Max grabbed his arm.

"Dad," is all he said. "We have to check on him."

I sprinted for the door, but as I reached it, Liam shoved me out of the *way so he could enter first. At the time, I remember being pissed off that he, like always, had to be first. In hindsight, I realize he was doing it to protect me.*

The second we got inside the store, a cop came over to us before we could round the corner.

"This is a crime scene, boys. You've got to get out of here."

"Our father works here," Liam said.

The officer's eyes flashed. Pity. I saw it before he shut it down.

"There's been a shooting," the cop said, speaking mainly to Liam.

"We just saw a guy run off," I said, pointing to the door.

The officer immediately sent another cop out to look. He also said he'd take our statements.

That's when Jared started to scream. I looked where he was looking. Blood. A trail of it.

I walked past the cop and followed that trail of blood right up to the counter. And then, I looked to my left, where Dad was being attended to by EMTs.

"Fuck, no. Dad." Jared rushed over and tried to take his hand.

"He's lost a lot of blood," one of the EMTs said. "He's unconscious."

"We need to get him into the ambulance," the other one said as they carefully lifted Dad onto a gurney.

Liam had me by the arm. "We'll follow them to the hospital."

We spent hours at the hospital. It was after two when the surgeon came out to the waiting room to talk to the four of us.

"I'm sorry," he said, that same look of pity in his eyes that the cop had. "We did everything we could. He's gone."

And in that moment, a part of all of us was gone also.

CHAPTER SEVENTEEN

Winter

Hunter's been acting distant.

When he first landed in New York, he was sweet and caring in our text exchanges, a conversation that he initiated. I didn't necessarily expect to hear from him so soon, but I so appreciated him reaching out.

But other than a brief, "Goodnight, Princess" after the New Orleans Fire crush New York, I don't hear from him again.

He's been eerily radio silent.

I text him a quick "congrats" after each win, and he either sends back a thumbs-up emoji or a "Thanks, Winter" with nothing else attached.

I waffle between fearing that something's wrong to thinking he's just taking his space and enjoying the time away with the guys.

Whatever's going on, it's not hurting his performance on the ice. The way he's playing is, for lack of a better word, a match to his team name—Fire.

Hunter's been locked in during the games in a way I've never seen him. I didn't watch all of his games over the years, and I don't know a ton about ice hockey, but I know some, and I definitely know enough to recognize when a player is completely, utterly dominant.

That's been Hunter throughout every game of this road trip.

He's owned nearly every possession.

He's played like his life depends on him scoring or helping someone else to score.

The last time I saw him this focused on the ice was the first game he played after his father's funeral.

Liam also seems extra intense. The two of them look like they could be beating their opponents by themselves. If Hunter isn't scoring, Liam is. And Hunter scores a lot.

Just one more away game—this time in Nashville tonight— and then the team flies home. I don't know if Hunter's arriving late tonight or tomorrow morning, and I haven't wanted to bug him with a text.

But I'm so excited to see him it's a bit unnerving. I've had Theo for company, and we've snuggled together for every game, and then he's slept at the foot of my bed at night. But I've missed Hunter something crazy. I can't deny it, certainly not to myself. And I find myself craving the games just so I can get a look at him. Is it nuts that I feel like I'm spending a couple of hours with him during every game? Yes, it most surely is.

Peyton and Ashley arrive at the townhouse to watch the game with me. Peyton left the morning after Hunter kissed me in public at the game to go with Scott on a visit to his parents. I used her absence as an excuse to put off Ashley whenever she tried to get me to tell her what was going on with Hunter.

I promised I'd fill her in but only when the three of us could be together.

"Okay. Let's just get right to it, shall we?" Ashley tosses her bag on the couch and throws her hands on her hips. Her jeans fit her like a glove, and her blue silk blouse is the perfect compliment. Her auburn hair is piled on top of her head in a messy bun, and she's wearing no makeup. Ashley is the epitome of a natural beauty. As usual, she looks like she spent hours getting ready but, in reality, spent about five minutes. "Peyton's here—check. I'm here—check. And you're here. So spill it."

Peyton puts down the take-out Mexican food she offered to bring and gives me a hug. "I guess I missed some things while I was away, huh?"

Peyton's hair is braided casually, and her yellow top and black pants are nearly outshined by her gorgeous strappy shoes. She looks nice and relaxed from her time away, so the opposite of how I'm feeling. I pick up the bag of food and invite them both to follow me into the kitchen.

"I'm not sure where to start," I say as I take out plates from the cabinet. "Hunter and I have always been undefined. You both know that. Nothing's changed there."

"Nothing?" Peyton asks in disbelief. "You certainly look different from when I left."

"What do you mean?" I glance down at my track pants and the red and gold Fire sweatshirt of Hunter's that I've fallen in love with. "I'm messy. See?"

"You're wearing your housemate's clothes." Peyton tugs at the hem of the sweatshirt. "Last I checked, people don't normally do that unless..."

"Unless they're fucking," Ashley sums up with a wide grin. "Oh, come on, Winter, just kill the suspense already, would you? I've been ridiculously patient this past week while I waited for our bestie to return home."

I take a moment to arrange the nachos that Peyton brought over onto a plate, which I then place on a serving tray I find buried in Hunter's pantry.

Finger food is very important to have on hand during a hockey game. It helps keep me occupied while I'm stressing over who has the puck and praying the other team doesn't score.

"Hunter and I..." I look up from the tray to find my two oldest friends watching me intently. "We kissed. More than that one time after the game."

Peyton's eyes brighten with interest. "So he's not 'just a housemate' anymore."

"Technically, he's your employer," Ashley says. "Right?"

"Yeah, that doesn't sound very good," I say. "I doubt the pet sitting agency had kissing in mind when they hired me to work here."

"Don't worry about all of that," Ashley says as if I'm talking about a little rainstorm.

I carry the tray over to the couch, and the three of us sit down with our food.

"I feel like I'm missing something," Peyton says to me as her dark eyes study me. "Am I?"

I let out a slow breath. "Yes. There's something I haven't told you. I wasn't ready to share before, but I am now."

I launch into what happened to me in New York, and I barely stop for breath until I've finished the story of my assault.

Peyton hugs me, and Ashley wipes tears from her eyes.

Peyton's eyes are now blazing with anger. "I knew you were hurting over something. I should have come right out and asked you what was going on."

"You practically did do that," I say. "But I wasn't ready to talk about it."

"Oh, Win." Ashley puts her arms around me. "How awful."

And I know she gets it—it hits so close to home for her.

Ashley is a total badass, but she came from a home of abuse, so it means the world when she says she's proud of me.

"The way you handled your home life growing up was so courageous," I tell her. "It's always inspired me."

"You know what's funny?" she says to me. "Hearing about your life in Manhattan and how successful you've been on your own helped me immensely. Moving there at eighteen was the epitome of courageous, Win."

I laugh. "I think it was more the epitome of clueless. I honestly didn't know any better. If I had, I probably would have been too afraid to go."

"You're so strong to have gone to the police," Ashley says. "Especially after he threatened you."

"I'll need even more strength if I'm called to testify," I say. "They're trying to bring him to trial."

"I hope that bastard gets convicted," Peyton says with feeling.

"Did you tell Hunt?" Ashley asks.

"I told him everything. He was amazingly supportive. He..." I trail off.

"He and you..." Ashley says encouragingly.

"We're...us," I say. "You know Hunt and me. We don't make anything official. It starts out as blurry and deteriorates from there."

"This sounds different than high school," Peyton says. "First of all, you had sex this time."

"How do you know?"

"I didn't. But you just confirmed my hunch." She laughs.

"Yay!" Ashley says. "That's a big step, Win."

"It is. Hunt's just...he can be so sweet, but then it's like he disappears inside his own brick walls, and I can't reach him."

"All the Storm brothers learned to protect themselves when their daddy died," Ashley says with a shrug of her shoulders.

Yes, they did. And Hunt as well as any of them.

The game starts, and we stop talking about Hunter and watch him play instead.

He kicks ass once again with two goals and an assist.

When the game ends, I hug Peyton and Ashley goodnight and sit back down on the couch with Theo. And I open up my laptop.

I've been working on my musical all week. Ever since Hunter and I texted that first night he was gone and I confessed my dream of writing my own musical, I couldn't get the idea out of my head. I adore musicals, but to write the score and book is a ton of work. Most musicals are adaptations, but I decided to try to write one based on the story that's been running through my

head. The score I'm going to need help with, but I have an idea
for that.

The one thing I know for sure is that it suits me to be in
charge of my own story. I write until I'm so tired I'm yawning,
and the next thing I know, I'm curling up on the couch, too tired
to even go to my bed to sleep.

CHAPTER EIGHTEEN

Hunter

When we touch down in New Orleans, all I want is to see Winter.

I wave good night to the guys and head for my truck.

Tomorrow at three pm. Precinct Five police station.

Liam's parting words run on a loop in my brain as I drive toward my home. And my salvation.

Winter.

I make it home in record time, throw the truck into park, and take the front steps two at a time.

I unlock the door and type in the security code. I walk into the living room, taking care to be quiet when I notice Winter asleep on the couch. Her laptop's on the floor, and Theo's curled up at her feet. They make a nice picture—a much better picture than the nightmare flashback from my past that's been circling through my head all week.

I put down my bag.

I need Winter too badly right now to just walk on by and go to my bedroom, but I'm not going to try to wake her.

All right, maybe I am.

I sit down on the couch next to her and gently run my hand over her midnight-colored hair that's tangled in a messy ponytail at the nape of her neck.

She's always been a light sleeper, and she opens her eyes. Those blue eyes that could cut diamonds. And that always see right through me.

She blinks.

She can tell. She knows I'm wound up about something, and worry crosses her face.

A silent acknowledgement passes between us. I'm sure she's wondering why the hell I haven't called her at all. The truth is, ever since Liam told me about the "person of interest" in our dad's case, I've been shutting everybody out. I get that's probably not the healthiest way to handle it, but I haven't felt capable of doing anything else.

Winter's gaze stays focused on me, and just when I'm sure she's going to pepper me with questions I'm not prepared to answer, she reaches a hand up and snakes it around my neck.

"I was tired of missing you," she says softly.

I exhale. Like always, Winter gets me. She knows when I need to talk, and she sure as hell knows when I'm not ready to.

I lean down and kiss her on the lips.

I mean for it to be light. A hello kiss.

It's not light, and it doesn't come off like a greeting. The kiss is raw and hungry and unfiltered. It's filled with pain and vulnerability.

Winter takes all of it, and she gives me nothing in return but care and love.

And God, I'm fucking falling for her all over again. But it's different now. It's better.

She shifts on the couch so I can lie next to her, and then she raises her leg over my waist and urges me closer. I'm rock hard, and I let her know it when I line myself up between her legs. She moans and starts tearing at my jeans.

Within seconds, we're both half-naked, and she's on her back, begging me to come inside her. I climb over her and pause.

"Are you sure?"

"Yes, I'm positive." Her eyes are hazy with lust, and I want her more than I've ever wanted another woman.

With a groan, I push inside her slowly. She's warm and tight and wet, and her nails dig into my back as she urges me to go deeper.

I've just spent ten days on the road in different hotel beds, all of them uncomfortable. I played in multiple hockey games where I fought guys against the boards and on the ice. My body is bruised, sore, and exhausted.

But the moment I sink into Winter and feel her arms around me, I feel rejuvenated. Most importantly, I feel.

If it were anyone else beneath me, I'd be using sex tonight to try to forget. To stop thinking for a little while, to stop feeling so that, for a short time, I can't hurt.

But I can't do that with Winter. I can't stop feeling with her. I never could. Winter Allen's not the kind of woman you fuck to forget. You don't fuck her to block out your life and all its problems. She's the kind of woman you make love to over and over again because she makes you feel alive. She makes you *want* to be alive. To reach for the stars.

Winter rotates her hips, and I nearly come right then.

I take hold of her waist and try to slow her motion somehow.

"I'm not gonna last, Princess," I bite out. "I'm so close."

"Me, too." Her blue eyes glaze over as she stares up at me. "Take me there, Hunt."

I pick up my pace as I start pumping in and out of her lightning-fast. She meets my every thrust, and my mouth covers hers as we cross the threshold together.

She moans out my name as my own orgasm hits me. Hot waves of ecstasy start at the bottom of my spine and explode throughout my body. I hold tightly to her hips as I come for so long I can barely hold myself up by the time I finish.

That wasn't just an orgasm. That was...shit. I don't know what that was.

I pull out and curl up next to her. "That was pretty intense."

Her laugh is muffled as she buries her face in my neck. "It always is with us."

"I know, but—" *But that was like nothing I've ever experienced.* "That felt more so."

She raises her head and strokes the week-old facial hair I've grown. "It did."

We both go quiet, but I don't take my eyes off of her.

Finally, I say, "What are you doing tomorrow?"

She narrows her eyes. "Why are you asking?"

I inhale sharply. "Because I have to go possibly ID my dad's killer."

Winter murmurs my name as she runs her hand up and down my arm. "Is that why you've..."

"Yeah." I kiss her head. "That's why I've been a shit friend to you this past week. I wasn't ready to talk about any of this, and I can't lie to you."

"I understand. But Hunt? You could have told me that by phone, and I wouldn't have pushed you to say more."

"I should have. I'm sorry."

"It's okay."

"It's not okay to shut you out without an explanation. But that's what I've always done, especially when it comes to family shit."

"I know."

"But I'm working on changing that."

"Hunt." Winter sits up and looks at me seriously. "I don't want you changing for me. I want you changing if that change makes you happier in your life."

She's wearing my Fire sweatshirt and nothing below the waist. Her black, shiny hair is half out of her ponytail after our vigorous lovemaking. Her cheeks are flushed, and she looks like a woman who's just come hard. She's never looked more beautiful.

I wrap my arms around her and stand up with her snuggled against my chest. "I get where you're coming from, but you're worth changing for, Princess. Let's go to bed. I'm not done hearing you call out my name when you come."

CHAPTER NINETEEN

Winter

A part of me wants to have access to the part of Hunter Storm that no one ever gets to see.

A part of me is terrified because I'm broken, too. I don't know that I'm strong enough to stand by this man—whose energy is so powerful—and help him heal when I'm still trying to heal myself.

But when he asked me to come with him to the police station, I didn't hesitate.

I know what it means for Hunter to let someone in even a little in regards to his father's death. I was touched he reached out for support and more than a little surprised.

But I'm determined not to let him down. I'll be strong for him, and I'll be there for him as much as he'll let me.

———

I wake up before Hunter the next morning. I glance at the clock. Only eight a.m.

But Theo's hungry. Every morning, he waits for me to open my eyes. As soon as he sees I'm awake, he starts purring. And moving. He stands up, stretches, and makes his way from the foot of my bed up to my head where he stops and lets out a full meow. If I don't get up and feed him, he meows again. Yes, he has me well-trained.

Hunter's heavy arm over my side is keeping me pinned firmly against him, so I lift his arm and slip out from under it. I'm completely naked, so I grab one of Hunter's oversized hockey jerseys from his walk-in closet. It reaches my mid-thigh and is seriously comfortable.

I'm going to miss stealing Hunter's shirts when I'm back in Manhattan.

The thought comes out of nowhere, and it makes me nearly stop in my tracks. The idea of leaving him is getting harder and harder.

I push the unpleasantness of it all out of my mind and walk into the kitchen to get Theo his breakfast.

After feeding the kitty and cleaning his litter box, I head back down the hall where I bump into a sleepy Hunter. He's wearing nothing but gray track pants that hang low on his hips, exposing the dark trail of hair leading to an impressive bulge. His dark hair sticks up on his head, and his green eyes look at me hungrily.

"Hey." He snags the hem of his jersey I'm wearing. "I was looking for you."

I steer him toward his bedroom.

"Still early. Let's go back to bed."

"Exactly my line of thinking." He follows me into the bedroom, and we snuggle under the covers together.

He slips his hand below his jersey where he finds me bare.

"Christ, Winter." He dips his head to kiss my mouth. "A Fire jersey *and* no panties? Are you trying to kill me?"

I lift the jersey to give him better access. "I love wearing your clothes," I tell him. "Especially your hockey stuff. Does that make me a jersey chaser or something?"

His other hand tangles in my hair as he kisses along my jawline. "No," he murmurs. "You're a jersey catcher, maybe."

"Are you saying I caught you?"

"Absolutely." He's got the jersey up over my breasts now, and I raise my arms so he can take it all the way off.

He lowers his mouth to my bare nipples, which are taut with need. When his lips close firmly over one nipple and he starts rolling the other one between his thumb and forefinger, my eyes drift closed from the overwhelming sensation.

I arch beneath his touch, and when I feel his thick length against my thigh, I start rocking into him.

All of a sudden, he flips us so I'm on top and straddling him.

"What are you doing?" I ask as I brace my hands on his ridiculously ripped abs.

"Do you want to lead?" His green eyes are hot with desire as he keeps his hands on my hips.

"Um..." Yeah? God, it's been so long since I've felt in control of anything.

"You prefer me to be on top," he says like he knows what I'm thinking.

"Okay." I move to climb off of him, but his hands lock onto my hips and hold me in place.

"Wait. Winter." His tone is serious. "I think you want this."

I think I do, too.

"I'm not very experienced with different positions," I admit. "I slept with a few guys in Manhattan, but it wasn't..." *Like this.* "It was always very vanilla."

"Vanilla?" His mouth quirks up.

"Yes." I shove at his shoulder, and he grabs my wrist and laughs. "You know what I mean—it wasn't very passionate."

"Why'd you date those guys then?" His tone is almost posses-sive, and I could swear he sounds...

"Are you jealous?" I say in disbelief.

"No." He says it fast. Superfast. *Too* fast.

"You are." I give him a look. "I heard about your partying side and all the women. So don't act like you could date and I couldn't."

"I'm not." His tense jaw relaxes. "Okay, maybe I was. I just don't like thinking of you with anyone else because I don't think anyone else gets you like I do."

The rawness of the confession catches me off-guard.

My irritation with him disappears.

"That may be true," I say.

"May...be?" he asks me, taking my chin in his hand.

"Is." I swallow. "That has always been true."

And with that confession, I lift my hips, take Hunter's hard length in my hand, and sink down onto him.

"Holy...fuck, Winter." Hunter growls out a slew of curse words as I take him all the way inside me.

"How's this?" I ask him.

"Princess, this is..." His fingers dig into my hips. "Incredible."

I don't move at first. My body isn't used to this angle, and Hunter's not exactly small.

"You can ride me." Hunter's emerald green eyes glitter with heat.

So much heat between us—I can't stop staring into his eyes.

"Ride me, Winter. At your pace."

With my gaze still locked onto his, I shift upward slowly and then back down.

"Jesus." Hunter shifts his hand to my ass. "You feel so damn good."

I shift up again, but this time I come down harder. The pressure inside is so intense that I let out a moan. A long moan. It sounds obscene, honestly.

I glance down at Hunter, whose eyes are squeezed shut. He looks tense.

"Are you sure you're enjoying this?" I ask him.

"Win, if I enjoyed it any more, I'd be erupting inside you

right now." He opens his eyes like it's an effort. "I love literally every fucking thing that you're doing. If you like it, don't stop."

His obvious pleasure breaks the dam of hesitation inside of me. I start riding him in earnest, moving up and down so his hard cock hits me over and over in the exact right spot. Hunter's hands on my ass urge me forward as he says in a halting tone, "Touch your breasts."

I pluck at my nipples which are hard as glass, and Hunter groans.

"So hot," he murmurs as he runs his hand down to my thigh.

I keep riding him furiously. "I'm so close. So close."

"Come for me, Win."

"I can't..." *I need you closer.* "I want to kiss you."

"Come here." Hunter tugs me down to his chest, and then he puts his arms around me. "Can you ride me this way?"

"I think so." It takes me a second, but soon I'm back in a rhythm.

Hunter's mouth covers mine, and I keep up the pace until I tire. And then, Hunter takes over, fucking me from below while I just hang on for the ride.

I clutch at his hair, and our tongues tangle together as he thrusts up, hitting me deep inside from this angle. His thumb drags down my tailbone and brushes between my ass cheeks, and...

I go off like a bomb. I cry out my release into Hunter's mouth, and he fucks me through my orgasm. Just as I'm coming down, he lets out a long groan, and I feel him explode inside me. And now I'm coming again.

"Oh God. Hunt!" I hold onto the short hairs on his head like they can somehow ground me.

I feel like I'm flying. In this moment, I really and truly feel invincible.

Because of my connection to this man, who I knew as a boy. Who I've always lov...

I cut off my own train of thought, nearly biting my tongue in the process.

I don't love Hunter Storm.

He's helping me out. He's being a good friend. That's it.

"Fucking hell, Winter." His hot lips land on my sweaty neck. "You're so goddamned sexy. You know that?"

"With you," I murmur into his shoulder. "With you, I feel all those sexy things you say I am."

"With or without me," he says firmly. "But I prefer with me."

I raise my head to look at him.

"Just wanted to make that clear," he says, his voice rough.

I suck in a breath, unable to break the eye contact. I want to be with Hunter Storm for a lot longer than this temporary time-line we've put on whatever it is that we're doing. I just don't know how to make that work or how to tell him.

All I can say is, "I feel the same."

———

Hunter

After reuniting last night with Winter, followed by this morning when she blew my mind in bed, I'm feeling slightly less edgy about what I'm about to do.

I still want to take a bat to whoever killed my father, but having Winter beside me as we walk across the parking lot of the police station calms me in a way I don't want to think too hard about.

I take her hand in mine as we get near the front door, and we're just about to enter when I hear, "Storm."

Still holding Winter's hand, I whip around.

Jared and Max are striding toward us. Their faces are grim.

"What are you two doing here?" I ask in shock.

"You seriously think we wouldn't come to try to ID our father's murderer?" Jared scowls at me.

Clearly trying to break the tension, Max grins at Winter. "Must be because Hunt's the youngest. He never seems to know as much as Jared and I."

Winter smiles, but she squeezes my hand, and I know she's letting me know that she's on my side.

Like he's just noticing, Max's gaze goes to our joined hands. "You two together now?" He raises an eyebrow.

"Seriously?" Jared says before Winter or I can answer. "You two are finally..."

"No," I say firmly. "I don't know," I add, and both my brothers crack up. "Shut up and focus on why we're all here."

At that moment, Liam peels into the parking lot in the black SUV he bought after Lulu was born.

He hops out of the driver's side and shuts the door behind him. The SUV beeps as he flicks his remote to lock the doors.

"Hey, Hunt. Winter." Like my other brothers, Liam's gaze immediately goes to Winter's hand wrapped in mine. "About time you two made it official. Or are you both going to deny it?"

"If no comment is a denial, then yes," I say curtly. "Like I've already said, let's stay on topic today."

Liam gives me a chin tilt before turning to Jared and Max.

"What are you assholes doing here?" he says. "I told you not to come. You'll get a team fine."

"We cleared it with Coach," Max says. "He said, and I quote, 'I hope you can ID that bastard and bring justice to your family.'"

Winter's hand tightens in mine.

I glance over at her. "You okay?"

She nods. But as my three brothers turn toward the door of the station, Winter tugs at my hand like she's trying to pull away.

"I don't belong in there, Hunter." Her blue eyes are as still as the lake I used to fish in with my dad. "You four deserve to do this in private. It's a family matter."

But I'm not letting her go that easily. "Do you *want* to come with me?" I ask her.

"I want to support you," she says. "However that works for you. What I don't want is to get in the way."

Liam's holding the door open for us. "Come on, you two." He looks at Winter. "You were there for Hunt on that shitty night. And for every day after for months. In ways I couldn't be. So don't you think for one second that we don't want you here."

Winter's eyes soften. "Okay. Thank you, Liam."

CHAPTER TWENTY

Winter

We follow the cop through the station hallway single file. Hunter and I sit on metal chairs across from Liam and Max while Jared paces between the four of us.

"Will you sit the fuck down?" Hunter growls at Jared.

"You know I don't deal that way." Jared scowls. "I need to keep moving."

After about ten minutes, the same cop returns. "We're ready for you," he says.

Hunter leans over and kisses me briefly on the lips. "Be right back."

"Take care," I tell him.

God, that sounded stupid.

"Good luck," I try again.

Still shitty as hell.

Oh, well. He's gone with his brothers—all four of them follow the cop down the hall and into a room.

While I wait, I cross and then uncross my legs. I stare at the screen of my phone and realize I'm reading things and not absorbing any of it. The knots in my stomach are so intense I worry I'm going to be sick.

This is personal for me. Mr. Storm may not have been my dad, but his death hit our entire community hard. To watch the four Storm boys become orphans was brutal. Thank God Liam had just turned eighteen and could file for custody of his brothers. The idea of them being separated still gives me chills. I don't think any of the four would have survived if they had been taken from each other.

As I continue to sit on the cold metal chair and wait, flashbacks of the night Hunter's dad died flood my brain. And my heart.

I was sitting cross-legged on my bed, wearing my favorite slouchy sweatshirt and worn blue jeans. I'd been staying up late all week, trying to learn my lines for our school's rendition of Rent. The pebble—honestly, it was a rock and Hunter's lucky the glass didn't shatter—hitting my bedroom window startled me so much I dropped my laptop on my bare foot. While I was hobbling off my bed, another stone hit the pane. I glanced out, and thanks to my dad's always-on security lights, I saw Hunter standing on our lawn. He was looking up at my window, and we caught eyes.

Even through glass and from a story up, I knew something was very wrong.

Hunter and I weren't *that* couple. We didn't go knocking on each other's windows in the middle of the night for a romantic rendezvous. We didn't sleep over at each other's houses or make out for hours after dark. We hooked up when the moment presented itself, and then we walked away like it was nothing. Even though that was a lie.

I threw my feet into sneakers, grabbed my backpack with my keys in it, and left my room. Closing my door quietly behind me so my parents would assume I was still in my bedroom, I crept down the stairs and out the back door.

Hunter was waiting. Leaning against the brick wall next to the door, he had his head down so that the hood of his sweatshirt blocked his profile.

"Hey." I reached for his arm. "What's going on?"

He turned toward me. His face was pale and his expression tortured.

For the rest of my life, I knew I'd never forget the stark whiteness of his skin against his green eyes, which were filled with the kind of pain that doesn't go away in a day. Or a year. Or a lifetime.

Hunter's eyes changed after his mama died when he was young. This time, though, they looked so gut-stricken I didn't know what to do.

"What's wrong?" I shook his arm. "What happened?"

"My dad." He held up his hands.

And that's when I saw the blood.

"Oh my God! Hunter!" I reached for his blood-stained hands, but he pulled them back. "Are you hurt? Should I take you to the hospital?"

"Already been there." His tone is a flatline when he says, "My dad was murdered."

I threw my arms around him, but he inched out of my hug. "Come with me to my house?" he asked me. "We had to talk to the police and give our statements, and my brothers are still at the hospital dealing with shit. I just needed..."

Our eyes caught and held.

I nodded. "Of course. Let's go."

He'd taken a cab to my house, and he had it waiting out on the street where it couldn't be seen. We walked across my lawn together and hopped into the cab.

When we got to his house, the first thing I thought was how eerily quiet it was as we stepped inside the foyer.

"Deadly silent," Hunter said immediately.

I jerked my head over to him. He shrugged like he was trying the words out to see how horrible they felt.

Then, he leaned over and gagged, barely making it down the hall to the lone bathroom before he threw up in the toilet.

I grabbed a washcloth, wet it with cool water, and put it on the back of Hunter's neck. His hands gripped the toilet seat so hard his knuckles were white.

"Hunt." I ran my hand down his back. "Let's get you into bed."

But he insisted on cleaning up first.

I followed him into the bathroom and started handing him soap and a clean washcloth from the linen closet.

"What if I can never wash off the blood?" His face was still so pale that all I could see were his green eyes glittering with grief.

I stepped closer and took the soap from him. "We'll get it all off. I'll help you."

It took several scrubbings to fully clean his daddy's blood off of him, and even then, we found more on his jeans.

"Jump into the shower," I finally said. "I'll put a pair of your sweatpants outside the door for when you're done."

I left the bathroom and rummaged through his drawer to grab his track pants. I left them outside the bathroom for him, and then I grabbed one of Hunter's t-shirts and a pair of his shorts for myself to change into.

When he came out, without him inviting me to stay and without me asking if I should, we climbed into his twin-sized bed together.

I kept my back to him and as much distance between us as I could at first, not sure what he wanted from me. But when I felt the bed shake, I rolled over toward him.

"Hunt."

He shifted to face me. The tears running down his face were visible in the moonlight that shone through his window.

I didn't know then that would be the last time I'd ever see Hunter cry about his father.

I scooted closer so I could take him in my arms.

His tears soaked through my t-shirt, and when he lifted his head and said so, my response was immediate.

"You think I care about that? I care about you, Hunt. Just you."

Nothing had ever felt more true or more right.

In that moment, I would have gladly given up Broadway for a shot at something real with Hunter Storm.

His hungry lips sought mine, and we came together in a clash of pain, confusion, and grief.

Within seconds, he'd pulled the t-shirt up and over my head. His hands cupped my bare breasts, his thumbs running over my nipples.

"Hunter." I bit back on a moan.

His eyes locked with mine. "You're so beautiful."

His mouth went to my neck, and he peppered me with kisses all the way to my breasts. His hands went to the top of the shorts I was wearing. He slid his fingers just inside the waistband and paused before glancing up at me.

His dark lashes framed his emerald eyes as he silently asked me for permission.

My breath was coming in short little gasps. I had never been naked with a boy before.

But I wanted this. Because it was Hunter.

I shimmied to help him ease the shorts down my legs and off. And then, I was bare to him.

He sucked in a breath. The rough pads of his fingers grazed the inside of my thigh...and then dragged up to my core. He brushed his index finger across me once, twice.

I bit my lip to keep from crying out. It felt good, so good, and I closed my eyes at the intensity of the sensation.

When I felt Hunter's thick finger slide deeper into my wet folds, I clenched in resistance.

I didn't want to resist him, but I tensed as my thighs shook. God, I wanted him inside me so badly. I could hardly breathe as I bucked up into his hand between my legs.

"Relax," he whispered. "I've got you."

He held my legs with his other hand so I wouldn't thrash, and

I took a long, slow breath as he gently moved his finger to my opening. I let out a low moan of approval, and Hunter's finger penetrated me.

Oh, Jesus. "Oh my God," I murmured as I felt him go deeper.

The orgasm hit me hard, and waves of pleasure pulsed through me.

I clutched at Hunter's arm and cried out. The sensations flooding my core were brand-new to me. I touched myself sometimes. But not like this. And I had never brought myself to orgasm before.

As I came back down to earth, Hunter kissed me. "Was that okay?" he asked.

"More than okay. That was...like I was flying." I rested my chin on his chest. "Can I touch you?"

When he nodded, I reached inside his sweatpants. I widened my eyes when my hand closed around his erection.

I ran my fist up and down the thick length, and Hunter's eyes slammed shut.

"Fuck, Winter. Feels so good."

All I wanted was to make him feel good. On a night when his entire life was blown apart with grief and pain, if I could help him for a few minutes, maybe he'd have one good memory to help balance out the horrible one that I knew he'd have to deal with for a long time hereafter.

He began thrusting into my grip. I kept up my firm movement until my hand was covered in his release and my name came out a whisper on his lips.

Before I'd even removed my hand, I felt him start to get hard again. I raised my eyes to his. Hunter's gaze caught mine, and I knew what he wanted.

I certainly knew what I wanted.

God, I wanted him so much that night. I would have given him all of me if he'd asked.

But he didn't.

After another hot as hell kiss and his hands cupping my

breasts again, he broke away and mumbled, "Sorry," before turning away from me.

I understood where he was coming from. It felt like a rejection, but I didn't even need to ask to know why he did it. He would say he pushed me away because he didn't ever want me to feel used.

I also knew the truth of why Hunter wouldn't allow himself to make love to me that night—he was terrified to open his heart again to anyone because he feared he'd lose them, too. I felt his fear when his hands shook as he ran them down my body. I felt his angst when he kissed me like I was everything and then abruptly shut down our connection.

And I didn't push him. How could I? I could only love him from the other side of the tiny twin bed we were sharing. I beamed as much love as I could over to him that night while he slept fitfully.

The funeral was quick and heartbreaking. My parents went, and they did their best to be caring. But when Hunter showed up at our house that same night, they didn't exactly roll out the red carpet for him. Not that their behavior stopped us from sleeping together.

And when I say sleeping together, I mean that literally.

Hunter couldn't sleep alone for a month. So, I slept with him. Sometimes we kissed. Sometimes we did a little more. Every time, he pulled back.

He threw himself even harder into hockey. All the Storm brothers did. And they started doing everything together. They were always tight, but now they were inseparable.

After a month of sharing the same bed, one night Hunter texted me that he was okay to sleep alone.

You sure? I texted back.

I've got my brothers here. That should be enough.

Okay. It was the right thing to do. I knew it was. I was preparing for my future, too. I had Broadway in my sights, and getting attached to sleeping with Hunter wasn't a smart idea.

Long pause before—

Thanks, Princess. I'll never forget what you did for me.

The text I sent back to him was one word that I hoped conveyed everything he meant to me.

Anytime.

————

Hunter

Liam goes into the room first, followed by Jared, then Max, and me.

The detective shuts the door and turns toward us before flicking the button to reveal the suspects.

"You men ready?"

The last time we did this, it was a different detective. He asked us the same thing with one distinction: "You boys ready?"

Because we were kids then. Innocent kids who didn't know what the fuck we were going to do without parents.

But this time, we're grown-ups. We've got houses and money and jobs. All those life things that terrified us back then are no longer concerns. And yet, as I stand in the same room I stood in with my three brothers all those years ago, the same emotions flood me.

Rage.

Fear.

Grief.

Just proving that all the money and success and notoriety in the world can't give us back our father.

But possibly, the man who did take him from us is behind that window. And, maybe this time, we'll have the chance to get justice and to close the book once and for all on what happened.

The detective raises the partition so that we can see in but the men in the line-up can't see out.

They stare right at us, though, and it gives me the creeps.

"They can't see us," Liam says quietly to the three of us.

"I know," we all say in the same quick way we answered him last time we were here.

I scan the line-up. I'd know the killer in my sleep. And yet, despite looking for him relentlessly, I never saw him. And the cops never found him. It was like he disappeared into the woods after shooting Dad and was never seen again.

Until—

"That's him." I point at the fourth guy from the left. "Right fucking there."

Liam's next to me. His arm's touching mine, and I feel him flinch. "Fuck, you're right. That's definitely him."

The detective whips his gaze over to us. "You're both sure?"

Max and Jared, in unison, bark out, "That's the killer."

"See that birthmark?" I say to the detective. "It's an exact match to what I remember seeing. The shape, the color, everything."

"He's the one we had our eyes on. We'll start by holding him for questioning," the detective says. "He's been on the run for years, and he's wanted in connection with several shootings. He's changed his ID, gone underground. He had some help hiding."

"From who?" Liam asks.

"He's a gang member." The detective shrugs. "Their network is large and goes beyond New Orleans. He'd come into the city and then disappear again. His father's the head of the gang, so he's connected."

I stare at the guy through the glass, at the man who took my father's life without thinking twice. A careless, cruel act that killed one man and changed the lives of his four children.

I want to kill him myself. Because no matter how long he goes to jail for, it won't change what he did.

I'm done with this. With all of it.

"I'll meet you outside," I tell my brothers.

I need to find Winter.

CHAPTER TWENTY-ONE

I find her waiting for me on that same uncomfortable metal chair she was sitting on when I left.

"Hey." I sit down next to her and take her hand.

All I want to do right now is touch Winter. Just like that horrendous night when my father died, Winter is the only person who can calm me when I feel like I'm going to explode.

"What happened?" she asks me.

"I ID'd him," I tell her. "We all did."

Her blue eyes widen. "Seriously?"

"Yep. They're holding him for questioning. So I'm going to pray they can pull a confession out of him."

She throws her arms around my neck. "Thank God."

I relax into her embrace. I pretend like I'm comforting her as she cries a little into my neck and then kisses me twice on the lips. Of course, we both know that's a lie.

Winter's taking care of me. She always has.

She raises her eyebrows. "You know what your brothers are going to want to do now, right?"

Shit. She's right.

"You can still see a lot of the city," Jared says. "They haven't built a tall building to block the view yet."

Liam, Max, Jared, and Winter all crane their necks in the direction he's pointing. I don't bother because I'm too busy looking up at the sky. The big, orange sun is sinking below the skyline, and the view is prettier than any building.

The five of us are sitting on the roof of my childhood home. Our legs dangle off the ledge. The roof is flat over the outdoor patio, and it's a one-story house, so we're only about six feet off the ground.

Max passes me the bottle of whiskey that all of us except for Winter are sharing. I got her to take one shot, but after that, she said she'd leave the drinking to the four of us.

"It's so wonderful you were able to keep this house," Winter says.

"It is," Max agrees. "It feels a little weird with none of us living in it."

Liam bought the house back from the bank as soon as he got his first paycheck after turning pro. It was his first big purchase.

His second was to pay for his three brothers to go to college. None of us made it through four years—we all got drafted young, and we were anxious to take care of ourselves financially so Liam didn't have to anymore.

The sad irony is that Liam was the only one of us who truly enjoyed studying, and I know he would have loved college. But life's not always fair, and Liam was the oldest and the one who sacrificed so we could all get what Dad wanted for us—play professional hockey and excel at it.

Winter leans over and kisses me. "I'm going to leave you boys to catch up for a while," she says. "I'll see you at home."

"Be ready because I have a surprise for you later," I whisper in her ear.

She smiles. "I'll look forward to it."

After she's gone, the four of us lie on our backs and stare at the darkening sky.

"Can't believe we caught him." Jared's words are barely audible.

"Doesn't change the past," Max says in his typical rough tone.

"No," Liam says. "But maybe it will help us bury this shit for good. The cop said he'd give us a call when they find out more." He glances over at Max. "You don't want to pass down all that anger to your kids someday, do you?"

"I don't plan to have kids, so that solves that problem," Max says with a chuckle we all know is meant to mask his pain.

"You don't want kids?" I ask him.

"Nope. And I thought you didn't either," Max says to me.

"Is that why you don't date?" I ask him.

His jaw tenses. I can see it from here. And he doesn't answer me.

Jared elbows me in the ribs. "Has your new housemate changed your mind about having your own family?"

I flip him off, but while they're all laughing, Winter crosses my mind.

Would I want kids? The answer to that is simple—only if Winter and I did the parenting thing together. She's the only woman I ever saw a future with.

"Are you two serious?" Max asks me.

I take a swig of whiskey rather than answer him. What am I supposed to say, that Winter and I are fuck buddies? Something tells me none of my brothers would believe that even though technically it's the absolute truth. But when I'm with Winter, I don't believe it, either.

"She's the only woman I know who can put up with your bullshit," Liam says. "She even came babysitting with Hunt the other night," he says to the twins. "And they were both great with Lulu." He turns to me. "You looked good all domesticated."

"Fuck off," I say to him.

But I felt it, too. Taking care of Lulu with Winter beside me —it felt easy. And far too comfortable. When she leaves for New York, I don't want to miss her the way I did the last time.

I already know in my gut that it's going to be far worse than that, though. We're connecting as adults, and with our past as a foundation—it's damn near addictive.

"Question." Jared sits up and looks over at me from the other side of Max. His dark hair is longer in the front, and it falls into his eyes as he stares at me. "I don't mean to get in your business, but something's been bugging me about the night we lost Dad."

"Okay." I have no idea where he's going with this, and I gesture for him to continue.

"How did Winter end up at our house that night?" Jared asks me. "Neither of you had your licenses yet. And I didn't think you called her before you left the hospital."

"I didn't. I took a cab to her house," I say.

"In the middle of the night?" Liam doesn't look over, but the surprise in his voice is obvious. "What if she didn't wake up when you knocked or threw shit at her window or whatever it is you two did?"

"I knew she'd be there for me," I say easily. Truer words were never spoken. "When I got there, I asked her if she'd come over. She said *of course*. She even—" I cut off.

But my nosy brothers' interests are piqued.

"She what, Hunt?" Liam asks me.

"She cleaned Dad's blood off of my hands."

"Fuck." Liam's tone is gruffer than usual. "You never told us that."

"None of your business," I remind him.

"Still," Jared says in an odd tone, one I can't decipher. "It's kind of a big thing to do for someone."

Yes, it's a big fucking deal. Only one of the million reasons why I missed Winter so damn much when she moved away. And why I've fallen so hard for her since she returned.

"Anyway," I say in an effort to bring the subject to a close. "After she helped me clean up, she stayed over. Nothing happened," I feel compelled to add.

I've thought about that night countless times over the years. How Winter was there for me. How her body melded to mine.

Thank God I didn't take it as far as I wanted to. That would have been wrong on so many levels. However, the truth then is still the truth now—I wanted Winter badly, and that night, it took everything in my power to stop myself from telling her that.

"Sounds like you two are right back where you're supposed to be," Liam says.

I glare at him. "Aren't you the same guy who warned me away from her when she first came back to town?"

"I've changed my mind," Liam says. "I was looking at you and Winter through jaded eyes. I think you two could be really great together."

His response is too honest for me to fuck with him. And the brutal candor of his answer is so clearly laced with pain about his own relationship with Cathy that I don't want to go after him. Given that, my only option is to stay quiet. Because fuck if I'm going to tell *anyone* how I feel about Winter before I tell her.

———

Winter

I'm relaxing on the couch with Theo, watching a lighthearted movie, when Hunter comes home.

"Hey, darling," he says as he walks into the living room.

Darling. I've missed the south. More than I've cared to admit. And I really missed the people. One person in particular.

Flipping around to face him, I reach out and touch his bicep as he joins me on the couch.

"How are you?"

Hunter blows out a breath. "I'm good."

I rub his arm. "How are you really?"

He shoots me a lopsided grin, the kind of grin that says he

knows what I'm asking but he's not really sure what to say. That's Hunter speak for—*I appreciate you pushing me, but I may not be ready to answer you yet.*

But then, he does answer me, and his response is stripped of any cover.

"Honestly?" he says. "I want to know why it took so damn long to catch him."

I feel the same way. "I often wondered why it wasn't solved," I say. "I thought about your dad endlessly, you know. About the four of you needing closure on his case."

"I didn't know that." Hunter shifts so our legs are touching. "I shouldn't be surprised, though. You've stood by me from the beginning on this. I would have completely lost it were it not for you."

I lean closer to him. "You healed on your own."

"Not true. I healed with you by my side." He reaches for my hand. "And in my bed."

I squeeze his hand. "I know you didn't actually mean that to be flirty."

He chuckles. "No." He pauses before saying, "I told my brothers what you did for me that night. How you helped me clean up."

"Hunt. It was nothing."

He brings our joined hands to his lips and kisses my knuckles. "It. Was. Everything. And I'm sorry I didn't thank you properly before now. I honest to God just wanted to forget that whole night."

"Of course you did. And I certainly wasn't waiting for a thank you."

"Doesn't mean you didn't deserve one."

His eyes fill with emotion.

"You're going to get through this next step," I say confidently. "Putting that horrible man behind bars...it's long past due, but I'm happy for you all."

"Thanks, Win."

I lean my head back against the couch. "How was the rest of your roof time?" I ask him.

He shrugs, and I hide a smile. The Storm brothers are so close-knit, but they like to pretend otherwise. I think it stems from their fear of loss, and my heart aches for all of them.

"Liam's a know-it-all, Jared tries to fuck with everyone about everything, and Max is still pissed off," Hunter says as he tugs my feet onto his lap.

"That sounds about right." I laugh. "But they all also have hearts of gold. Just like you." I smile at him. "You know that you're my favorite Storm."

He raises an eyebrow at me. "Oh yeah?"

"Most definitely."

I sigh as he starts massaging my feet. "That feels amazing, Hunt."

"Good." He keeps going as he says, "I need to get you all limbered up for your big night."

I flick my gaze to his. "What big night? I'm not leaving this couch."

"Oh, yes, you are."

"Where?"

"We're going to the Riverway. Oliver's performing, and I told him we'd stop by. Peyton and Ashley are going, too."

I've been pretty much avoiding live music in New Orleans since I've come back. It hits a little too close to home.

Hunter's watching me. "I don't want to push you, Win."

I give him a look. "Yes, you do."

His lip quirks up. "Okay, you're right. I do."

I kiss his cheek. "I appreciate your concern. But I'm really okay."

"Then why did you look terrified when I mentioned going to Oliver's show?"

I put my hand on Hunter's knee. "Because. I'm still getting over the fact that I've bombed my last few auditions. So I guess the idea of taking in a live show is a bit overwhelming. But I'm game. Let's go."

"You're sure?"

"I'm sure." I'm not at all sure, but I figure I can pass the time chatting with Peyton and Ashley.

Hunter tugs at my ponytail, using his grip on my hair to hold me in place so he can give me a perfectly dirty kiss. His teeth tug at my bottom lip until he can slide his tongue inside my mouth. I arch my neck to get as close to him as possible.

He finishes the kiss by murmuring in my ear, "That's just a taste of what I have in store for later in bed."

And now I'll be officially going to the Riverway with wet panties.

———

Oliver's on stage when we arrive. The place is packed with wall-to-wall people. Hunter, Peyton, Ashley, and I grab stools at the bar so we can chat with Blaire while she works.

Oliver's got his guitar with him, and he breaks into one of my favorites right away. I forget about everyone I'm with while I tap my foot to the music and enjoy his performance.

He sings several songs in a row, and the crowd is really loud in its applause. So loud that I miss whatever Oliver says next.

Peyton turns to me with a big smile. "I had no idea!"

"Wait." I feel a nervousness starting in my stomach even though I don't know why. "What?"

Before Peyton can answer me, Oliver calls out into the mic, "Winter Allen, come on up here!"

Oh, shit. I turn toward Hunter. "You neglected to mention this part, Hunt."

He shakes his head. "I didn't put him up to this. I swear, I had no fucking clue. I thought you couldn't sing yet because of your vocal cords."

I can't do much. But I sang in the shower the other day, and the pain was gone. I texted my doctor about it. He told me to go slowly but that as long as I didn't strain, I could try again.

"I think physically I'm okay," I tell Hunter. "Just not emotionally."

By now, the crowd is involved. Someone's started a chant of, "Winter, Winter," and people are more than happy to add their voices to the mix.

"Oh, God." I look at Peyton helplessly. "I am so not ready for this."

Ashley puts her arm around me. "Remember what we were discussing the other day about courage? Maybe this is one of those moments."

Maybe so.

Oh, what the hell.

I step off of my stool.

Oliver meets me on the edge of the stage. He extends his hand and helps me up as he shoots me a mischievous grin.

I grab his mic out of his hand and say into it, "This is called manipulation, Mr. Black."

He reaches for a second mic and hooks it up. "I prefer to call it good-natured trickery, sugar."

I laugh as he starts strumming the guitar. My legs are shaking from the adrenaline rush of being on a stage again, and I still can't face the crowd, so I keep my gaze glued to Oliver's hand as he strums the guitar strings.

"You know this one still, right Win?" He repeats the chords and looks over at me.

I recognize the tune right away. It's an old country song, one Oliver and I used to sing together way back in high school.

"Yes, I still know it." I grip the mic like it's a lifeline. "Ready when you are."

He starts into the first verse, and I use the beautiful sound of his voice to ground me. Oliver is so talented, so gifted. He could have easily left New Orleans to perform elsewhere, but he prefers to be at home in the Big Easy.

And maybe I do, too, I realize as I join in with him on the chorus. I spent my entire childhood trying to get out of New Orleans. But once I got away, life wasn't all bliss and rainbows like I imagined it would be. And I don't mean just the last six months.

New York City can be a lonely place. Broadway is ultra-competitive, and you never really know who you can trust. I formed friendships, but a lot of times, we were ultimately competing for the same roles. I felt like I was constantly running, constantly chasing my dreams across the hard New York pavement and through the gloomy, smelly subways. Frequently, I came up short.

Living in New Orleans again, I'm starting to wonder if maybe my life was already good before I left. Yes, I needed to stretch my wings and learn to fly. But learning to love where I grew up is important too, and now that I have my wings, maybe I really can have it all.

As we finish the chorus and I dive into the second verse solo, I risk a glance out at the crowd. They're cheering and singing right along with me. I shift my gaze across the room until I lock eyes with a certain green-eyed man who's the reason I'm in this bar tonight, who's had my back from the very beginning. Hunter winks at me, and I sing the rest of the verse—all about someone who's your first, last, and only—directly to him.

And when we get home later that night, he definitely makes good on his earlier promise—he has *a lot* in store for me in bed. After three orgasms, we fall asleep in each other's arms. Yes, I'm definitely falling hard for Hunter Storm. So hard that when I receive unexpected news from New York City, I truly don't know what to do.

CHAPTER TWENTY-TWO

Hunter

A week passes with no word from the police. We've got a short road trip coming up, and at Winter's advice, I force myself to put thoughts of dad's murderer into the back of my mind. She wanted me to have a successful trip, and she was right when she said my dad would want the same thing.

Little did we know that as soon as our team reaches our first destination, not thinking about the events of my father's death would be pretty much impossible.

"The detective called." Liam leans against the Denver Alphas' visiting team lockers and speaks in a low tone. "I just took the call out in the hall."

I freeze in the middle of putting on my shoulder pads. "And?"

"The asshole confessed." He accentuates the three words slowly and with an extra southern twang to them.

I drop my pads to the tiled floor. "Shit."

We take seats on the wooden bench in front of the lockers. No one else is around us.

"His name's Sal O'Brien." Liam speaks so quietly I have to bend my head to hear him. "He said it was a robbery gone wrong. He didn't plan to shoot Dad. He just wanted to scare him and grab everything in the cash register."

No.

I don't want to hear the rest.

But I have to.

I look into my brother's hard eyes. "But—"

"But Dad fought back. He said the guy would have to go through him to get the money. He said it wasn't his and he wouldn't let him get away with it."

Fuck. Dad, why?

"But Dad started to open the drawer anyway. I think he was trying to tempt him while he pressed the emergency alarm at his feet. Remember that thing, how we were wondering why it didn't work?"

My hands are in fists, and I feel like I'm literally going to destroy something. I feel like I *need* to destroy something.

I force my voice to stay level when I say, "Yeah. Was it broken?"

"It was *disconnected*. The Sal asshole said he could see Dad tapping his foot over and over on the ground, and Sal freaked. Thought it was some sort of signal. So, he fired a shot. But he swears he didn't mean to actually hit him. He just wanted to scare him."

"So he was a shitty shot on top of everything else. *If* he's telling the truth."

Liam's face fills with pain. "I hate that he suffered. I hate it more than anything."

I try to cover my own rage as I put my hand on his shoulder. "I know. It's not fucking fair. Any of it."

And I'm going to break something. I grit my teeth and try to catch a deep breath, but I'm coming up empty.

Liam holds up his phone. "I'm going to call the twins before I get dressed. Be right back."

An idea hits me, some way to channel these feelings.

"Hey," I call to him.

He looks back over his shoulder. "Yeah?"

"Let's dedicate tonight's game to Dad. He always wanted to visit Denver, remember?"

"He wanted to see the mountains," Liam says, a half-smile crossing his face. "Good idea—let's do it."

After he leaves, I can't concentrate on anything. Normally, I joke around with Murph and a few of the guys. I go through a mental warm-up for the upcoming battle. I have my preps down.

One thing I never do is call Winter this close to game time.

I prefer to see her afterward when I can relax and really connect to her.

But I won't be seeing her tonight because we play Arizona tomorrow, and we won't be home in between.

My finger hovers over the touchpad of my phone.

I should wait to talk to her. Focus on the game.

But my heart isn't listening to my mind. Not this time.

She picks up on the first ring. "Hunt? Doesn't your game start soon? Is everything all right?"

Her unselfish concern and care for me hit me straight in the chest. More than that, my body's reaction to her voice is palpable.

I relax. I stop nearly hyperventilating, which I've been on the verge of since Liam told me the news. And, I stop wanting to put my fist through the metal locker.

I'm in love with her.

It's the first time I've allowed myself to admit that.

I love Winter so much that I nearly tell her.

But it's not the right time for that. I don't want my feelings for her to hold her back from returning to New York. I don't want to be that guy. And I don't know that *I'm* ready for what saying those words will entail.

So, instead I say, "Everything's fine. I just wanted to hear your voice."

"That's sweet, Hunt."

"And, Liam heard some news."

"Oh?" Her voice rises. "You mean about the case?"

"Yep. The guy confessed to the murder of our father."

She exhales both a breath and a stricken sound at the same time. "Oh, Hunt. Honey, I'm so sorry I can't be there with you."

"Me, too. But I'll be home tomorrow night late."

"Did you get details?" she asks in a nervous tone. "I'm assuming you did?"

"We did. They're pretty...brutal."

"I'm here for you," she says softly. "If you want to talk after the game tonight, no matter the hour, call me."

"I will. Will you be watching the game?"

"Of course."

"Well, Liam and I are gonna put on a show, darling. So get ready."

"I'll be glued to the television set," she promises. "Be safe. Kick some ass."

———

Playing a hockey game as a tribute to your late father brings up all sorts of emotions.

Anger, yes, because of the way he died.

But I didn't expect to feel the grief, too.

The air in the arena is cool as usual, and I relish the cold-as-ice feel tonight because that's what I'm feeling in my veins. Cold and lethal.

I want to wash that fucker's murderous face out of my head for good.

Liam and I line up on opposite sides of the ice like always. But this time, when he leans forward, he turns his head briefly. I catch his eye, and he tips his chin in the direction of Denver's goal.

I nod back at him.

And then, it's on.

As soon as the ref drops the puck, Liam fights for it. He has control within seconds, and he slaps the puck over to me.

I'm in the zone as I skate past one defender and then keep the puck away from another. I back up, eye Liam skating down the middle, and as soon as he has a finger-width of space, I zip the puck over to him.

I don't even wait to see what he's going to do.

It's like I know.

I shift further left, dodging the defenseman in my path, and as Liam makes it look like he's going to shoot, instead, he passes it back to me.

I don't bother to take possession of the puck before firing my stick through it. The goalie's out of position, and the puck shoots by him and over the goal line.

I raise my stick to the heavens.

Goal One.

For Dad.

We do it three more times.

Twice, Liam scores, and I get one more myself. On two of our goals, the puck actually looks like it's flying wide of the net, but then at the last second, it snakes inside the crossbar. It almost looked like someone's hand gently nudged or guided it there.

I've never believed my father was watching our games before, but apparently, I haven't paid close enough attention.

When the game ends, Murph and Dean wrap their arms around my brother and me.

"What the hell got into you two tonight? I've never seen you both perform like that on the *same* night," Murph says.

"Retribution," Liam says simply.

"Redemption," I add.

He and I look at each other and then up at the ceiling.

I think my father was here with us tonight. Maybe he always is, and I haven't taken the time to feel his presence.

———

Winter's lips are on mine the second I walk into my townhouse at an ungodly hour the next night. Hell, it's really morning.

"It's after three a.m.," I say to her between kisses. "Shouldn't you be sleeping?"

"I was waiting for you," she says simply.

That's all I need to hear.

Everything I've felt the past forty-eight hours, all the emotions that I've been keeping to myself...they all come out.

I put my mouth over hers in an urgent kiss and back her up against the wall. She meets me more than halfway, giving as much as she's taking.

I lift up the t-shirt she's wearing of mine and tug at her underwear. As I slide them down her legs, she pulls at my tie.

I practically tear the tie off of me before unbuttoning my dress shirt. I don't even bother to take it off as I unbuckle my belt and unsnap my pants.

Winter releases my erection from my boxer briefs, and I lift her up. She fits perfectly with me, and her legs lock around my waist as I brace her against the wall.

I want her so badly I'm shaking. I can't wait to be inside of her, but I need to make sure she's ready.

"Do you want this?" I ask as I run my finger through her wet center.

"God, yes." She grips my waist tighter with her legs.

I try to go slowly, but she's so wet that I slide all the way inside of her in one motion.

And fuck, I'm so hard that with just one thrust, I feel close.

I force myself to slow down and look into her eyes. Her beautiful, blue eyes that see all of me. Not just Hunter Storm the hockey player, but Hunter Storm the boy who lost his parents, and Hunter Storm the man I am now.

Our gazes stay fastened on each other as I drive in and out of her. Every time she moans, I get closer, and I grip her hips to angle her more tightly against me.

"Hunt..." Winter's eyes grow unfocused and more dilated. "I'm going to...oh God, Hunt...I'm..." Her fingernails dig into my shoulders as she cries out her release.

Her eyes never leave mine.

Watching Winter's eyes change as she comes is the hottest thing ever, and I drive into her harder.

"Fuck." I drag my finger across her hip and flick her clit lightly. "Win, I'm coming..."

She moans loudly as I release inside her, and as I feel her clench around me, I realize she's coming for a second time.

I start kissing her as we're both coming down from our highs.

We kiss for a long time, and I realize how deep in I am with this friends-who-fuck thing we have going on.

"Let's go to bed and talk properly," she says in my ear. "I want to hear all about your dad and what the police told Liam."

Friends-who-fuck is clearly the wrong way to describe Winter and me. The truth is—

I'm in love with her, and she's leaving.

But I don't want to rock the boat when neither of us seems certain as to what the future holds.

"Let's do that," I say as I kiss her cheek.

CHAPTER TWENTY-THREE

Winter

The next month and a half pass quickly. Hunter and I grow closer, spending as much time as possible together.

He seems more at peace now that the killer has been found and is in prison. When he first told me, he was angry and in shock, which I would have expected. And that game he played—holy crap. He and Liam looked like one person as they played that game for their daddy. I was so proud of them, and as I watched it, tears streamed down my face.

But once the shock wears off over what the murderer did the night he shot and killed Mr. Storm, Hunter seems to relax. He's more open, more willing to be vulnerable with me. We have some good talks, and I find myself really wishing I weren't leaving.

I'm falling for him. Like really falling for him. Honestly, I love him. But I don't know how to broach the concept of dating because Hunter isn't into commitment. Plus, I'm going to be leaving eventually. And what would we do then?

I channel my attachment to him through sex. Which we have a lot of. Like every night he's in town.

And when he goes away on a team road trip, I miss him. Also a lot.

But now, we don't lose touch. He calls me every night even if it's just to say goodnight before he has to hop on the plane to fly to another city.

I put my loneliness into working on my musical, which is coming along.

One day, I stop by to visit an old friend.

Mr. Les Anderson was my first piano teacher. He taught me the classics and how to read sheet music and write songs. His lessons were my musical foundation. But he also taught me how to play the songs I wanted to sing. From rock to pop to country, we sat side by side at his piano and played for hours.

I went by after school when all my friends were hanging out or doing homework, and Les gave me invaluable training for my future. He had lived it. He used to be a director on Broadway, and he'd walked away to slow down and have a family.

I didn't understand his choice then, but I certainly have a better grasp of it now.

I walk through the French Quarter and stop outside a burnt orange building with a green arched doorway and matching shutters on the windows. The second story has the quintessential New Orleans cast-iron balcony with the same green shutters and an American flag hanging from the window.

I push open the door.

I see Les right away. He's sitting at the piano, and he's got his back to me. His hair is white now, and he's a little more hunched, but he's still playing. Still singing, too.

"Hello, old friend," I say as I walk across the room.

Les turns around on the bench. His entire face lights up when he sees me.

"Winter Allen. My dear." He stands up and opens his arms.

I fall into them.

"My Winter," he says. "Welcome home."

The tears come so fast I'm not expecting them.

"Now, now." Les reaches for the box of tissues on his desk. "Here you go."

I take a tissue and wipe my eyes.

Les leads me over to the two hard-backed chairs by the window. "Let's sit and talk."

I wasn't planning on telling him everything.

But I do.

I think it's why I waited so long to come see him. In the back of my mind, I knew I couldn't see Les without sharing my whole story.

Because Les Anderson has always been my surrogate grandfather. He was the man who helped me get up the courage to move to New York City. He said it would be hard but assured me I had what it took. And even though I made good on his faith in me, I'm ashamed I haven't gotten any roles since the assault. It makes me feel weak.

"You're the opposite of weak, my dear." Les takes my chin in his hand. "Remember that. Sometimes, things happen, and our priorities change as a result. That's not weakness. That's listening to our hearts."

I reach into my bag. "You always seemed to know where I was going with something before I actually told you. Along those lines, I've been working on something."

Les takes a look at the musical book on my iPad. "This is a good start," he says. "You've got something good here."

I flip through the pages on the screen so I can show him the score I've been working on. "Will you help me with the parts I'm stuck on?" I ask him. "I'll credit you as the primary songwriter."

"Absolutely not. You're over halfway along already."

"I'm crediting you," I say stubbornly. "I won't let you help me otherwise."

Les's blue eyes twinkle. "As obstinate as always, Winter. I knew that trait would get you far in Manhattan." He stands up. "Let's go sit by the piano together and get to work."

Les and I play and write for hours. We work until it's dark outside and I've forgotten about anything but what I'm doing inside his little music studio.

When we're done, Les is as excited as I am.

"I'm going to send this to my manager," I tell him. "See what he thinks."

"Just remember Broadway can be wonderful, but it's not the only way," Les says as he walks me to the door.

"What do you mean?" I ask him.

"Maybe you want to figure out how to make your own path here."

I stare at him. "Here as in New Orleans?"

Les smiles. "We've got a lot of talented residents in the Big Easy. You could do something with that musical right here."

"But shouldn't I use the connections I have on Broadway?" I ask him.

"If you'd like to, of course," he says. "I'm not steering you away from your dreams. I'm letting you know you're not stuck."

I hug him goodbye and grab a taxi to take me home. The French Quarter isn't safe at night, and no matter how short of a walk it is, I know I'm safer to be driven home than to walk alone.

I scroll through my phone from the backseat of the taxi. Hunter left me a voicemail, saying they landed in Houston and I can call him back whenever.

I'm smiling from hearing Hunter's voice when my phone rings.

Pat Buckman, my manager.

Butterflies shoot through my tummy. This would be the first time I've heard from Pat since I left.

He has no reason to be calling from Manhattan. *Not unless...*

I answer the call. Before he can say anything, I say, "Hi Pat. I have some exciting news."

"Me, too," he says in response.

Wanting to get my news out first, I start to tell him about the musical I've been writing.

"I know the industry prefers adaptations, but this story is fresh and contemporary," I say quickly. "It's a romance and has all the elements of a love story, but the heroine has a redemptive storyline, and she survives a physical attack. I think it will play well on Broadway or Off-Broadway."

"Forget that for now." Pat's voice is brisk but it can't hide the excitement beneath the surface. "I've got something better."

"What is it?"

"How does landing an audition for your dream role sound?"

I lose my air. "Wh-what?" I force out before sucking in a deep breath.

"Summerset Nights is having open auditions."

Summerset Nights. The mother-daughter musical Mama and I used to watch together when I was a little girl. Playing the daughter in that musical had always been her dream for me. And it had been my dream, too. At least, I thought it was. Now, I'm not so sure.

Pat explains how they've opened up the show to new talent. "And I've worked my magic for you and secured you an audition."

"When would I need to be back in Manhattan?"

"The new cast won't start rehearsals for a few months. Right around when you're scheduled to return anyway."

"Wow." I swallow. "Pat, I can't guarantee I'm ready for a live audition. I'm sure you remember how my last few have gone."

"That's why I convinced them to let you send in a taped audition."

"Seriously? That's amazing."

"I'll email you the details. Get started practicing ASAP. You can video your audition and send it back to me. Okay?"

I know how this business works. *I'll think about it* is not an option. You're either in or you're out, and I honestly don't know which I am. But I can't tell my manager that right now. So I give him the only answer he'll accept. "Okay."

Hunter

"Hey, do you think I should have a hot tub installed?" Murph asks from his hotel bed.

We're in Houston as part of our road trip. We don't play until tomorrow, and practice already finished for the day.

I don't take my attention off the sports countdown on the television. "No clue."

"It could liven up my house parties," he says. "I was thinking of putting it by the pool."

"Sure." I stare mindlessly at the sports co-hosts as they rattle off stats from the hockey games that were played today.

"What's up with you tonight?" Murph asks me. "You're not even listening."

"I never listen to you," I say jokingly.

"How're things with Winter? I thought you guys were doing well."

"We are." Except I called her hours ago and haven't heard back, which is unusual for Winter not to even send a text.

Looking for a distraction, I turn my head toward Murph. "I think you should get the hot tub."

"Yeah?"

I shrug. "Why not? You could use it in cold weather, right?"

My phone rings and I grab it without checking the caller.

"Oh, hey," I say, disappointed when I hear Jared's voice and not Winter's.

"Don't sound so happy," he says sarcastically.

"Murph's getting a hot tub," I say in response.

"Oh yeah? Ashley suggested it," he says, and I can hear the

amusement in his voice. "That girl loves the water. I think she's half mermaid."

I smirk. "Maybe you two could have some fun with the hot tub when you're in town."

He curses. "Ash and I don't vibe that way."

"The fuck you don't," I say. "I saw your chemistry at the Riverway. We all did."

"True story," Murph calls out from across the room.

"You don't get it." Jared pauses. "Shit, never mind. I've got to go anyway."

And I've got another call.

Winter.

I exhale in relief and swipe the screen. "Hey, gorgeous."

"Hey, Hunt," Winter says in a friendly tone. A forced, friendly tone.

Something's off.

"What's wrong?" I ask her. "Hold on, I'm going to find some privacy."

But Murph jumps up. "I'll be back. You want anything from the tavern next door?"

"Chicken burger and salad," I say to him.

He gives me a thumbs up and disappears out the door.

I wait until the door clicks closed before I return my attention to the phone. "Talk to me, Princess."

She lets out a heavy sigh. "It's a good thing. Really."

"What is?"

"My news."

Dread shoots through me. *She's leaving.*

"News?" I try to say the word lightly.

"Yeah. My manager called a little while ago. I was on my way home from visiting Les Anderson."

"That's great you saw Les. How is he?" Better to focus on the innocuous part of her story first.

"He's good. Really good. He and I worked all afternoon on the musical I'm writing. He was so incredibly helpful and supportive. And I was so excited when I left his studio, and that's when Pat called me. I tried to tell him about what I was working on, but he said none of that mattered because he had just snagged an audition slot for the role of a lifetime for me."

My breath catches in my throat. "Summerset Nights."

A long beat of silence follows.

"Yes," she finally says, her voice completely neutral and giving me no fucking clue what she's feeling. "Summerset Nights."

I force a smile onto my face even though she's not here to see it. "That's good news. Right?"

"I don't know. I mean, yes, it should be. And six months ago, I would have killed for this opportunity. But..." Her voice sounds so sad when she adds, "My mama was the one who took me to see Summerset Nights when I was a little girl. It was her dream for me, and somewhere along the way, it became my dream, too. But now I don't know what I want."

"When would you need to audition?"

"That's the thing. Pat arranged it so that I can do the audition from here. New Orleans. I can tape it and send it in."

I don't like the feeling that sweeps through me at this news. It's relief that she's not leaving yet. Which is fucking selfish of me. Because if Winter's dream is to play this role, then she deserves to.

I mentally punch myself in the nuts for my selfishness, and then I say to her, "I know that if you want this, you'll make a kick-ass audition tape. And don't let that asshole stop you from trying, either."

She releases what feels like a pent-up breath. "Thank you, Hunt. I knew you'd make me feel better. I think...I think I should go for it."

"Good," I say. "I think that's awesome. I'll be home tomorrow night after the game. I can help you prepare if you need me to."

"I don't think I can wait until then. Do you have a few minutes now to hear what I'm thinking?"

I settle back against the hotel pillows. "Of course. Lay it on me."

For the next half hour, Winter reads the script to me. At first, she's tentative while she finds her own voice inside that of the character. But by the time we go to sleep, she's nailing it.

"You've got this," I tell her. "You're ready."

CHAPTER TWENTY-FOUR

Winter

The next day, I videotape my audition for the lead role in Summerset Nights and send it in to Pat. He tells me it could be days before we know anything.

So, I put it out of my mind. And when Hunter walks in the door at two in the morning, I greet him like we've been apart for months instead of a week.

He picks me up and carries me straight to his bedroom where we proceed to make up for the days of abstinence that we missed. He tells me how much he missed me while he's inside me, on top of me, and beneath me. After that, we curl up together and talk before drifting off to sleep.

It feels like the kind of reunion real couples have.

When we wake up the next morning, Hunter tells me he's taking me out.

I smile as I get dressed, realizing I look forward to hanging out with Hunter clothed just as much as Hunter naked.

Because the truth is that Hunter and I haven't just been having sex since I've been back in the bayou. We've also gotten closer in other ways, ways that are seriously testing the rules of our *friends-who-fuck* agreement. We talk a lot. And we explore

New Orleans together, treating this time I'm in town almost like I'm a tourist who needs to see everything before leaving. Acting like Hunter's helping me to sightsee is a way to pretend that we're not going on dates apparently.

We don't say that, of course.

It's nice. More than nice. It's romantic and real at the same time. I feel like I'm getting to know Hunter all over again as an adult, and I didn't realize how much I missed having him in my life until he was back. The idea of leaving him—well, it floors me when I think too hard about it. So, I try not to. But turning in that audition tape was a reality check for both of us.

I saw it in his eyes the second he came home last night. As we were falling asleep, he asked me how it went. I said I'd sent the video to Pat, and Hunter kissed my head and said he was proud of me. Then, we said goodnight.

And now, as we walk down the street toward the French Quarter, he says, "When do you think you'll hear?"

"Pat said it could be a while," I say. "I honestly have no idea how long." Not wanting to stay on the topic, I smile as I see where Hunter's leading me. "Café du Monde again?"

"I thought you love that place."

"I do. You know I do. It feels a little bit like it's become our place."

There's been many a morning the last month and a half that Hunter and I have gone to Café du Monde for beignets.

Today, we luck out. The line isn't as bad as usual, and before too long, we're seated outside at a table with our breakfasts.

"God, I've missed beignets," I say as I devour my food. "I literally could orgasm over these sugary treats."

Hunter's green eyes darken. "Really." He holds up his hand for the check.

I grab at his hand. "Stop," I say, laughing. "I'm not ready to leave yet."

He grins. "I like seeing you happy, Win."

I like being happy. Before coming home to New Orleans, it

had been a long time since I'd woken up relaxed and actually looking forward to the day ahead. Lately, I'm actually getting out of bed with a smile on my face. And not just because Hunter got me off so good I can barely remember my life before we started having sex on the regular.

My smile slips when a woman approaches our table. Her attention is clearly fixed on Hunter, and she doesn't acknowledge my presence at all.

"Hi, sugar," she says to him. "Been a while."

Hunter's expression goes from relaxed and smiling to instantly on guard.

The other patrons don't typically bother us while we're actually eating. As we're coming and going, Hunter will often get asked for a selfie or an autograph by a little kid or a teenager, and he always complies.

I've had some people recognize me as well, but ever since that first night out at the Riverway, I haven't gotten stressed out about it. Maybe because I told Hunter the truth about New York. I also think it's because I'm with him so much, and I get to see firsthand how well he handles having fans. His fans are a lot more diehard than mine, and yet he's able to calm them down right away with a friendly word and a smile.

But this woman who's standing at our table does not seem like a random fan. She's got platinum-blond hair and is tall and thin. She could be beautiful if it weren't for the fact that her tan is sprayed on, her makeup is way too thick, and she has a terrible vibe about her.

She's solely focused on Hunter, and I could be mistaken, but it looks like they have a...um, history.

She places her perfectly-manicured hand with red nails on his arm. She does it in a possessive way, and then she angles her body to block my view of her face.

"How have you been? Lonely?" she purrs.

Hunter shoves his chair back to get some distance from her. "Not at all," he says with an obvious look toward me.

That changes the energy swirling around the three of us. Now, this woman is forced to turn her head and actually *look* at his dining companion.

Whatever she sees doesn't seem to concern her. She throws me a snide smile and then returns her attention to Hunter.

"Well, I've been lonely. Lonely for you," she says, putting her hand back on Hunter's arm.

This time, he reaches across the table and grabs my hand, which has been frozen in place with a fork in it this entire time.

I drop the fork and it clatters onto my plate, breaking the sudden silence.

"Hunt..." I start to say.

But he's already talking. "Deb, meet Winter."

Deb's expression turns sour like she just ate a lemon. "She's what's keeping you warm at night?"

"Every. Night." Hunter spells out the words slowly. "I have no room for anyone else, Deb."

Deb glares at me. "You don't deserve him."

I just raise my eyebrows. "I think Hunter can be the judge of that."

"I don't deserve Winter," he says, his eyes only on me now. "But I'm a lucky guy that she's giving me a shot anyway."

I let the warmth of his words and his hand on mine seep into me.

Deb gives a huff and storms off.

"Sorry about that." Hunter's cheeks are pink.

"You're embarrassed," I say to him in astonishment. "I don't know that I've ever seen you embarrassed."

He frowns. "Yes, I'm embarrassed. That was shitty of her. She never had any claim over me. We didn't ever date."

"We're not dating, either," I say stubbornly.

"What we're doing may not be definable, but it's meaningful," he says. "I dare you to say I'm wrong."

I flush with heat. "Of course it's meaningful," I murmur. "It's just...we said we're not in a relationship."

"We did say that." His eyes fix on mine.

"And..." And I can't have this conversation right now. I feel too raw. So, I go for something less personal but which stings nonetheless. "You must have slept with half the city of New Orleans, Mr. Storm."

He flinches. "That is absolutely not true," he says, and I know I've hit a nerve.

"Hunt." I gently rub his hand with my thumb. "I didn't mean it to come out like that. I just...Peyton told me about your reputation."

He lets go of my hand to tug at the hair on his head. I've never seen him so agitated, and I wait quietly for him to decide what he wants to say.

"Yes," he says finally. "I've had my share of women, but I didn't sleep around the way people think."

"So you had...what? A few select women on speed dial?"

He shifts uncomfortably. "I had women in my life I could call when I needed to..."

"To fuck." I say the words flatly.

"Winter, I told you I don't date." His green eyes are piercing as he stares at me like he's begging me to understand something.

"I don't get it," I say in confusion. "What are you trying to tell me, Hunter?"

"I'm telling you that I've never been able to get close to someone romantically. I'm not a snuggle-after-fucking, talk-under-the-covers kind of guy. I guess I'm not built that way."

"But you do all of that with me," I say.

"Yes, I do," he says, his tone raw and frustrated. "You know you're the only woman I've..."

He stops short, and my pulse picks up. But like him, I'm not sure I want him to continue his sentence. It's too scary to feel what's going on between us.

Instead, I change the subject.

"You have tomorrow off, right?" I ask him.

He nods, exhaling, and I can tell he's as relieved as I am to talk of something more casual. "Rare day off. With our big road trip coming up, Coach decided to give us a break after today's practice, which will be fucking brutal."

"So what do you do when you don't have a game or a practice?" I ask Hunter.

"I like to get out in nature and hike."

"Really?" I never knew Hunter to hike.

"Yeah. I got into it a few years ago during the off-season. I just needed to get out of the city, and I found my way to a trail."

"That's amazing."

"Not real intense hiking—that's hard to find around here. I just usually pack a snack and get out of town for the day. It clears my head. I can hear myself out there better than in the city a lot of times."

"That sounds nice," I say because it does. Learning who Hunter is now fascinates me, and the best part is how much I still like him. How much we still enjoy hanging out.

"You want to come with me tomorrow?" His eyes brighten. "I know of a great place about two hours out of the city in Mississippi. The weather's supposed to be sunny with no rain expected."

Hiking with Hunter. That sounds like something couples would do.

Like he can read my mind, he quickly adds, "Before you go back to New York, I want to make sure you spend some quality time outside of New Orleans. Get your feet down and soak in the southern countryside."

Yet another activity we're passing off as a non-date.

And I'm in.

I'm so far in I don't know how I'm going to back out when it's time to go.

"I'd need to be back by seven. I'm meeting Peyton for drinks."

"Sure. We'll keep good track of the time."

I guess we'd better keep good track of the time. Time is

passing quickly in the Bayou, and before I know it, these non-dates with Hunter will be just a memory.

———

After we finish breakfast, Hunter heads to practice. I snuggle on the couch with Theo and my musical book, but when I hit a snag, I put my work away and head for the kitchen.

I've been wanting to do something nice for Hunter after all he's done for me since I've moved home.

I eye the clock. Practice ends about ninety minutes from now. I'm full from breakfast and relaxed, and I've missed baking. I used to bake with my mama, but once I moved to New York City, I pretty much gave up cooking altogether.

I'm going to change that right now.

Hockey players aren't big on sweets, especially when they're in-season, but I know Hunter loves a good dessert every once in a while. And I know exactly which one.

So I take out a mixing bowl, turn on some music, and search Hunter's kitchen for the ingredients I'll need to get started.

———

I've just finished frosting the cupcakes when Hunter walks in the front door.

"What smells so damn good?" he asks as he steps into the kitchen.

I clean my hands on a dishcloth and give him a hug. "I made cupcakes. Healthy cupcakes," I add quickly. "Well, healthier. I substituted honey for sugar. And I know you have to watch your fat intake when you're playing, but I thought you deserved a little treat after how hard you've been working, and..."

His eyes are misty with emotion. "You remembered," he says as he curls his hand around the back of my head and kisses me long and hard.

I'm breathless when he finally lets go.

"I did," I say. "Cupcakes were what your mama used to always make for you boys when you were little. You and I had that in common—it's probably the one happy thing I can remember doing with my mom."

He grins. "You know I'm going to eat one now. And then, in about ten seconds, I'm going to eat another."

I reach for a cupcake and place it on a napkin.

"Here you go."

I grab one for myself, and we take seats on the couch together.

Hunter bites into the cupcake and immediately groans. "So fucking good," he says with a full mouth.

He's so sexy right now, and I snuggle closer to him as I bite into my own cupcake.

It is good. Rich and decadent, and the frosting is delicious.

"I've missed this," I say.

"Baking?"

"Eating whatever I want. We didn't eat a lot of desserts in New York," I say. "All my friends were in the business, and we were so worried about looking good for auditions or for whatever role we had at the time."

Hunter finishes off his cupcake and heads to the kitchen for another.

He calls over his shoulder, "You're gorgeous, Winter. You deserve to be happy, no matter your number on a scale."

Hunter always loved my body. Whether I'd gained five or ten pounds or was on another stage diet in high school, he never wavered in his attraction to me. I missed that kind of unconditional acceptance when I was away, but what's really sad is that I couldn't give that kind of acceptance to myself.

It's time to start. I finish my own cupcake and watch Hunter devour his before he even leaves the kitchen. I smile as he walks back toward me. When his ass hits the couch next to me, I climb on top of him.

"You're right," I say as I nibble his earlobe. "I need to treat my body well."

He reaches for the zipper on my jeans. "Let's start with me treating you well."

"You always do," I murmur, already feeling myself light up.

"I have a few more ideas up my sleeve."

His fingers slide inside my waistband and right into my panties. Within seconds, I'm riding his fingers as he brings me to the edge of climax. When his thumb circles my clit, my orgasm hits, taking me by storm. I close my eyes and drop my forehead to his shoulder as I ride out the bliss. My body feels limp when I finally open my eyes.

"We're not done, darling," he says as he kisses me.

But before he can try to give me another amazing orgasm, I drop to my knees in front of him. I reach for the snap on his jeans.

"Winter."

I know what he's looking for, and I raise my gaze to meet his.

"I want this, Hunter," I assure him. "I'm good. More than good."

He leans his head back against the couch cushions. "Then so am I."

He doesn't say anything while I unzip his jeans and take him out. But when I lean forward and lick his thick length, he lets out a guttural groan.

"Christ, that feels good."

When I take him into my mouth, he jerks his hips and calls out my name. I glance up to find his eyes on me. They're dark green and liquid with heat.

I keep sucking him, not stopping until he's bucking against my tongue and calling out my name. I climb up into his lap, and he wraps his arms around me.

"I vote we go get dinner and then continue where we left off on this couch," he says against my lips.

I vote the same.

———

Hunter's sleeping when I slip out of bed later that night and return to the living room. I can't get the book for my musical out of my head.

Les's help was invaluable with the score, and I want to fully finish the entire thing before I find out about my audition. I don't know why, exactly; I just feel like I need to have my passion project done. I'm not quite sure what to do with it when Pat was so unenthused, but maybe between Les and me, we can come up with an idea.

I've been working for a while and have completely lost track of time when I feel a hand on my shoulder. I look up at a shirt-less and sleepy-eyed Hunter. He was naked when I left him, but he's put on his track pants, and he takes a seat next to me on the couch.

"What are you doing up?" he asks me.

"Trying to finish the book portion."

"Can I see?"

I show him what I'm doing, and then I show him the score Les and I came up with.

"It's not quite done, and it's really rough, but it's getting there," I say proudly. "I don't know if anyone else will love it like I do, but I don't really care right now."

Hunter's wide awake now. His eyes shift between me and the work laid out on my lap, almost like he's just realizing something important. "I've never seen you this passionate about something."

His statement surprises me. "What about my dream to move to NYC and make it on Broadway?"

"That was different. With that, you were driven and determined as hell. With this, you just seem so...happy."

Huh. I never thought about my Broadway dream that way before. But Hunter's description tracks with me. It makes everything make sense in some weird way.

I tap his bare chest over his heart. "So hockey is your dream *and* your passion."

He nods. "Yeah. I got damn lucky."

I lean my head on his broad shoulder. "I'm glad. You deserve all the luck in the world."

He kisses me. "So do you. Come on. Let's go get some sleep."

CHAPTER TWENTY-FIVE

"You ready for our hike?" Hunter says the next morning.

I sleepily open one eye to see him sitting at the edge of the bed. He brushes a hair off my face. "You look beautiful." He gestures to the bedside table. "I made breakfast."

I glance over at the tray of scrambled eggs and toast. "Thank you. But it's so early."

He chuckles. "Babe, I have practice this early a couple times a week."

"My job involves late nights but not usually early mornings." I stretch my arms out from under the comforter.

Hunter scoots into bed next to me and props the pillow against the headboard. "You always were a night owl," he says as he picks up the tray and hands me my plate of food.

"True. I always loved when I got to stay up late for a school play I was in." My phone starts buzzing on the nightstand.

Hunter goes to grab it for me, but I put my hand on his arm.

"Don't worry about it. I'll check my messages later. I'm sure it's just my mother wanting to confirm our family dinner tomorrow night. No one else would call me this early on a weekend."

We enjoy our breakfast and then get a little distracted after eating when Hunter braces himself on top of me.

"Do you want to have sex?" he asks with an adorably sexy grin.

"I thought you wanted to hike," I say teasingly.

"This won't take long," he promises as he sucks on my neck. "If you're interested."

"I'm definitely interested," I say as he kisses me behind my ear. "Fuck me, please."

He enters me easily, lifting one of my legs into a bent position so he can go even deeper inside me. "Oh, fuck, Winter." His voice is all low and rough, and I love it. "Every time we do this..."

"Is better," I say, finishing his thought for him. "God, keep doing that, Hunt..."

Never taking his one hand off my leg, he drives in and out of me with abandon.

"Give it to me," he mutters. He shifts so he can snake his hand between my legs to brush my clit. "All of you, Win. Let go."

I come so hard I pull the sheet half off the bed.

As he follows me with his own release, we both collapse on the mattress.

"You ready to hike now?" Hunter mutters against my damp skin.

I laugh. "I feel like we just worked out."

He kisses my neck. "It will be a different kind of exercise."

I link my fingers through his. "Okay. But I need to shower first."

———

Black Creek Wilderness is about two hours away in Mississippi. Hunter and I pass the time talking. About anything and everything. Except for the deadline that's looming before us. That we don't discuss.

We do talk about my love-hate relationship with Broadway,

though, which feels like Hunter's roundabout way of trying to figure out where my head is at.

"I was lonely in Manhattan," I admit. "Kind of ridiculously lonely, honestly."

"What about your work colleagues? I thought you might bond with a few of them like I have with some of my teammates."

"It's not really like that," I say. "You guys are all on the same team, literally, and we're competing against each other. With the plays, you do get close with the cast, and that feels very familial. But then, whatever show you're working on ends its run, and you don't see the cast anymore. Not unless you make a point to meet up, and we're all just so busy..." I trail off.

Hunter's quiet for a few seconds. "I get it," he says at last. "It's like if I kept getting traded. Makes it hard to maintain relationships."

"Right. Exactly. And then there's the whole looks thing, which is so stressful."

"You're the most gorgeous woman I've ever known—inside and out," he says with feeling. "And you can try to argue I'm biased, but come on, Win—you won 'Most Beautiful' our senior year of high school. You're not exactly hurting in that department."

"I know. I'm very blessed, and I don't say this in a shallow way, but there are a lot of beautiful people in the world of entertainment. I've seen women—and men—who have perfect bodies starve themselves for a role or because their manager told them to lose fifteen pounds. It's a very real aspect of the business. And God forbid one media outlet say something negative about your size or figure—it's hard to ignore when it's in print for the world to see. We don't even deal with paparazzi like television actors do. They have it much worse."

Hunter shakes his head. "Everybody is so judgmental. Why can't people just accept that everyone is born different and we're all okay as we are?"

The sun is shining brightly when we begin our nature hike. The light breeze is a welcome relief as we get deeper into the woods. The pines and oaks are all around us as we walk quietly down the path. When we reach the creek, we immediately take off our sneakers and dip our toes in the water.

"So beautiful," I say. "Goodness, it's warm." I take off my sweatshirt and tie it around my waist.

"Let's stop and eat," Hunter suggests.

He leads me down the trail toward an open area. As we walk, I pull out my phone to take a picture.

That's when I see who texted me this morning, a text I forgot to check before we left the house.

"Crap." I stare at the message from Pat like I can decipher the meaning.

"What is it?" Hunter says as we take seats on a flat rock and open up our little backpack containing two peanut butter sandwiches. It's a sunny day, but that's not why I suddenly feel heated.

"My manager tried to reach me this morning. He wants me to call him ASAP."

The relaxed expression on Hunter's face diminishes. "You should call him then."

I nod and walk about ten feet away for some privacy before pressing Pat's number.

He answers on the first ring. "Where the heck have you been?"

"I'm on a nature walk," I say. "What's going on?"

"We got a quicker answer than I expected," he says cryptically.

"And..." I say.

"And you got the part, sweetheart! Congratulations."

Time slows down. The creek in front of me keeps flowing, and the pines sway gently in the breeze, but time almost seems to stop. I stare across the water at the utter lack of people. It's a strange dichotomy that I'm here in the middle of nowhere when I get the news I'm about to be on stage in front of countless audiences.

I wait for the burst of excitement I always get when I'm cast in something. Whether it's winning a small part or filling in for the lead, I always gave myself a mental fist bump whenever I got good news. But right now, I feel more numb than anything else. And I'm not sure why.

But I can't tell my manager that. He worked hard for me to have this opportunity, and I don't want to sound ungrateful. "Thank you," I say to Pat. "That's unbelievable to hear."

"There's also been a change in plans—it's going to be a limited run show. I didn't get the details on exactly how long the run will be, but I did learn that you'll need to return to NYC right away. Day after tomorrow at the latest."

My heart plummets.

"What? Why? I thought it wouldn't be for a few months."

"The director changed his mind. He wants to rotate the new cast in next month, so all of you will need to be in town, learning your lines and your marks."

"Pat..." I bang the back of my hand into my forehead. "I don't know if I can do that."

"Of course you can," he says, misunderstanding me. "You're strong enough now. I can hear it in your voice. You sound better than you have in years, frankly."

"Because I'm home," I say. "Once I leave New Orleans, who knows what will happen?"

"Sweetheart, you don't have a choice in this one. If you want the part, and I know you do, *this* is your moment. Make or break."

I take a deep breath. "Okay. I'll see what I can do for flights and text you later."

When I return to Hunter's side, he raises his eyebrows. "Good news?"

I take my seat next to him on the rock and tell him I got the part.

He wraps me up in a warm hug, and I melt into his arms.

"That's great," he says as he pulls back to look at me.

He's genuinely supportive, but his voice sounds off.

"You don't sound excited," I say.

"I am excited," he says. "As long as you're following your heart."

"Of course I am," I say sharply.

His eyes roam my face. "You just seem...I don't know—stressed? Like maybe Pat's more excited than you are about this."

I shake my head. "Not true."

He points to the notes sticking up out of the backpack. They were ideas I thought of for my musical, and I had us stop on our hike so I could jot them down.

"Could you play the lead in this musical you're writing?" He taps the notes.

"Yes," I say. "Technically. If I can get someone to produce and direct it. I need connections, and Pat didn't seem interested. And I don't have those kinds of connections on my own."

"Who says you need Broadway? What about Les Anderson? He's got a ton of connections in New Orleans."

I stare at him. He has a point. "I just can't think about this right now. Pat said he needs me to fly back to New York the day after tomorrow."

Hunter blinks. "Day after tomorrow. You're leaving that soon?"

"I have to." I cross my arms over my chest. "I don't want to leave so soon. I'll make sure the agency finds a replacement to take care of Theo."

"Winter. This isn't about Theo. You and I both know that."

Hunter's eyes shine so green as he searches my expression. I reach over and gently run my hand through his dark hair. "I know."

"I support whatever you do, Princess."

We're acting like we're breaking up. And when he reaches for my hand, it's bittersweet.

I clench my jaw as we lock eyes. "I have to take the role. I'll forever kick myself if I don't."

"I understand." He leans in and brushes his lips softly over mine. "No matter how far apart we are, I'm always here for you. Remember that."

I do. Hunter's always been there. He also gets me. The me that no one else sees. And right now, I read his face just like he read mine—he doesn't think I'm happy on Broadway. He'd be right. But that role...

Like I told him, I can't pass it up. So...I guess I've made up my mind. I'm going to fly to New York in two days.

As soon as we make the drive back to New Orleans, while Hunter's out grabbing us takeout for dinner, I book a one-way ticket to JFK Airport. I send my flight details to Pat.

A thumbs-up emoji is all I get in return.

New York.

I'm going back.

I feel stronger than I have in years.

I feel healed.

I'm going to miss everything about New Orleans.

But I'm going to miss Hunter something fierce.

———

Hunter

Winter and I sit in my truck as it idles at the curb of the airport.

Stay, I want to say. But I would never ask her something so unfair.

She turns to me, and the pain in her eyes is my first clue that she's not any surer of how to say goodbye than I am. "This was supposed to be easy."

"I know." I shoot her a grin. "You asked for friends with benefits. That should have been easy to deliver."

"It was," she says. "But somewhere along the way, it stopped being just an easy..." She bites her lip and looks at me with flushed cheeks.

I chuckle. "An easy fuck? Sugar, you were never that to me. You never could be."

"Hunt, you know you've always meant the world to me. But the sex *was* easy," she says.

"I guess when you know someone as well as we did, getting to know each other as adults just kind of fell into place." I cup her cheek in my hand. "I'll miss you, Princess. My house is going to feel awfully quiet when I get home tonight."

A single tear leaves her eye, and I catch it in my hand.

"Don't cry." I wrap her up in my arms. "You're following your dream. That's nothing to be sad about."

She presses her lips to mine. "You're worth crying over, Hunt. Being with you has changed my life. You truly healed me. And I can't thank you enough for that."

I love you.

Instead of words, I kiss her long and hard. When she steps out of the truck and I watch her walk away, emotion clogs my throat. I put the truck into gear and drive off, realizing this is the first time since the night I lost my dad that I've allowed myself to truly grieve for someone.

CHAPTER TWENTY-SIX

Winter

My alarm goes off for I don't know how long before I reach out my hand and bang it until it stops beeping at me.

I open one eye and check the time.

Ten a.m.

I've got rehearsal this afternoon, but I need to go over my lines this morning.

I force myself out of bed and into the shower. This bathroom is beautiful; thanks to Pat, my entire living space feels luxurious. One of his other clients took a job in Los Angeles for a guest role on a popular television show, and her two-bedroom was lying vacant.

Pat talked her into giving me a great deal. In other words, rent is still ridiculously expensive, but now I can make it work. My salary as the lead in a popular Broadway show is impressive. It's the most money I've ever made in my life.

My cast members are friendly and inclusive. I wouldn't call us besties because it always seems like everyone here is one stressed-out moment away from a catfight. But we get along, and that's been a huge relief.

My phone rings as I'm stepping out of the shower. I brace when I see Peyton's name flash on the screen.

"Hey," I say to her in a guarded tone. "How are you?"

"I was going to ask you that," she says with a laugh.

"I'm fine," I say quickly. "Tell me about you."

"I've been telling you about me every time we talk, and then you say you have to go before we get to you. So, I'm going to go fast today—I'm great. Scott's great. New Orleans is great. But what about you?"

I stare out the window of my high-rise apartment building. All I can see in the distance are more high-rises. When I look down, the cars zipping by look like ants from this distance.

"I'm fine," I say again. "Work is good. The musical is everything I thought it would be."

"So why do you sound so miserable?" she asks me.

I knew she'd see right through me. That's why I've kept our phone calls so brief whenever she's called.

"I don't know," I say finally. "I guess because I miss Hunter."

"Speaking of, you two haven't talked at all?"

"No. We can't do long distance. It's Hunter and me—I don't know, I guess whatever it was we had when I was home was never meant to last."

"Or maybe it was," she says confidently.

"Peyton. Ash said the same thing when she called last night. You two are delusional. Hunter Storm is not a relationship guy. He told me so himself."

"Hunter Storm never had you in his bed night after night," Peyton says. "I bet he misses you. And you know what I heard? He lives alone."

"What? Hunter can't live alone. He doesn't play well when he does." I don't mention where his issue stems from, although Peyton could probably guess.

"Well, he is. Cathy takes care of Theo when the boys go on road trips. She isn't thrilled about it, but Hunter hasn't found someone else he trusts yet. And the crazy thing? He's still playing at an MVP level. Living alone isn't screwing up his game anymore."

"That's so good to hear." I smile wider than I have since I left New Orleans. "I'm thrilled for him. I've tried to catch a few of his games, but my rehearsals are really intense right now, and they're always running late into the night. I know his stats are still off the charts, though."

"Win?"

"Yeah?"

"What's really going on?"

I sigh. "I'm not enjoying this, Peyton. Being back. Being the lead for what I thought was my dream role. I feel so ungrateful."

"Maybe you'd rather be happy than a star," she says.

"But this was the plan," I say. "This was always the plan."

"Maybe your plans have changed. Maybe you've changed."

Maybe I have.

And just like that, I know what I have to do.

————

Hunter

Liam and I drive home from the airport in his truck. We just crushed Dallas and clinched the division in the process. I had one of the best games of the season with three goals and an assist.

All this good shit going on, and I'm in a crappy mood.

"What's up your ass?" Liam growls as we stop at a light.

"Nothing. Fuck you." I look out the window and smile when I see the storefront of Les Anderson's studio.

Everything these days reminds me of Winter. When I come across a hair tie that she left behind in the bathroom. When I smell her shampoo on the pillow she slept on in my bed. When I find her favorite jar of almond butter still in the refrigerator. God, I miss her. And like a stubborn ass, I haven't called her once.

"You're a dumbass, you know that?" Liam turns off the main road and onto the side street toward his house. "Why'd you let her go?"

"This is the role of a lifetime for her," I say. "What did you expect me to do—stop her from living her dream?"

"You're even dumber than I thought," Liam says. "I wasn't talking about holding her back. I was talking about staying together even while she's in New York."

I turn away from the window and look at him. "Like a long-distance thing?"

"Yes, you stubborn fool. A long-distance 'thing.' God, and she puts up with you?" He chuckles.

"I don't know if I can do that," I say as I mull over the concept. "Long-distance."

"You haven't even so much as looked at another woman since Winter left town. You're seriously worried you're going to cheat on her?"

"No, not at all. I just mean that I can't figure out how we'd work between New York City and New Orleans. Not to mention all the travel that hockey entails."

"If you analyze how a relationship is or isn't going to work, you'll never get past the starting gate," Liam says. "Just ask yourself this—do you love her? If so, stop fucking around and go get her."

Christ. He's fucking right.

———

Winter

Rehearsal goes extra late tonight. Good thing the New Orleans Fire had the night off so I didn't miss another game. I stare down at my phone the entire cab ride to my apartment. My finger hovers over Hunter's contact information.

I want to call him and hear his voice.

I settle for a text.

How are you? I miss you and Theo.

The message goes through, but I don't hear back from him.

The taxi pulls up to the curb outside my building, and I pay the driver and hop out.

I'm walking slowly toward my door when I see a figure sitting on the front steps. It's dark, and the shadows of the nearby oak tree block his face from view.

Hoping it's not some guy looking to get into the building when he doesn't have a key, I pick up my pace as I plan to scoot past him. I keep my head down and take a wide angle so I don't need to get close to him.

When I'm a few feet away, I hear, "Hey, Princess."

I look over at the man who's in the middle of rising to his feet. As he steps out of the shadowy backdrop, I see him.

Those unmistakable green eyes that look at me like lasers; a strong jaw with a five o'clock shadow; a smile playing around his lips, and one hand running through his dark hair. His dark suit and white shirt look sexy as hell.

"Hunter!" I hurl myself into his arms, and he catches me.

We cling to each other for a few seconds, and when he finally puts me down on the ground, I can't stop smiling at him.

"You look so good," I say.

"So do you." He touches my cheek. "You're tired, though."

"I am." I'm exhausted, actually. I didn't realize how much until just now. I tilt my head and take him in. "What are you doing here?" I gasp. "You'll get fined for missing practice tomorrow! You can't stay!"

"Relax." He puts his arm around my shoulders and guides me inside my building. "I talked to my coach. It's all good. I'll be back in time for practice. I never changed out of my travel suit from the game earlier today. I just went straight to the airport."

"You weren't at the airport?"

He runs his hand across his jaw. "I was at the airport. Then, Liam and I started for home. We were almost there, but we were talking...about you, and..."

My heart comes up into my throat. "You were talking about me?"

"Yeah. Liam helped me realize what an idiot I was in letting you go."

I freeze in the middle of my apartment lobby. "He did?"

"He did. I..." Hunter shoves his hands into his pockets and tilts his chin toward the elevators. "Can we maybe go up to your apartment and talk?"

"Oh." God, I'm so flustered. "Yes. Of course. Let's go."

We head into a waiting elevator car, and I press the button for the nineteenth floor.

"Winter." Hunter's eyes hold mine. "Here's the thing: I love you."

I stare at him. "You do?"

He nods, his serious gaze holding mine. "I've loved you for a while. I just didn't want to hold you back, and I didn't want to fuck up what we had, and...well, I was a coward. I should have told you before. I love you so much, Win."

A love declaration in an elevator. I don't think I ever pictured this moment with Hunter. I never allowed myself to. But the truth is that I think I've always loved him.

I reach for his suit jacket and pull him closer. "I love you, too, Hunt. Honestly, I loved you when we were teenagers. I didn't let my heart speak too much on the matter, but you were always it for me."

His eyes darken as he swallows hard. "You've always, always been the only woman for me, Winter Allen. Nothing has ever changed that." He puts his hands on my hips and tugs me closer to him. "I want to make this work. Long-distance. We're not kids anymore. We can do this."

"We can," I agree. "But we don't have to."

He furrows his brow as the elevator comes to a stop and the doors open. As we step out and head down the hall toward my apartment, he says, "I don't get it."

"I'm coming home," I tell him. "To New Orleans."

His brow creases with concern. "But the show—it's your dream."

"It *was* my dream," I correct him. "I have bigger dreams now. Like being happy."

I unlock my door, and we step inside.

"Are you sure?" he asks me. "It's a lot to give up."

"I'm going to stay through the limited run of this show," I say. "Because I owe my younger self that closure. But then, I'm packing up and leaving Broadway for good. It's what my soul needs. You were right—my musical is my passion. I want to write my own roles and songs from now on. And I don't want to do that living in a city where I have no ties and where I feel like I have to join the race or I'll be run over. I want to slow down and actually enjoy life again."

"I'm happy for you," he says, his green eyes lighting up. He picks me up and swings me around. "You'll kick ass at whatever you do."

I wrap my legs around his waist. "I've missed you so much. I've tried to keep up with your games but it's been hard. I know you're still a scoring machine, though."

He brushes his lips against mine. "True."

"What about living alone?" I ask him. "Has that been hard?"

"You know what?" He kisses me lightly. "You said I helped you to heal. You did the same for me. I don't have a housemate right now. And I've been okay. Other than how much I want you back home with me. But no nightmares or scoring slumps."

"I think it's because you got closure when the killer was caught," I say. "I'd love to say it was because of me, but I don't think that's the truth."

"Both things are true," he says. "I'm a better man with you in my life, Winter."

"You're sweet." I kiss him back.

"Where's your bedroom?" He pats my ass. "I want to make up for lost time before I leave tomorrow."

I point him toward the hallway. We barely make it through

the doorway of my room before we're in a full-on make-out session.

Hunter has both our clothes off faster than I can blink. He backs me up against the wall and lifts me up. As he slides into me, I know this won't take long. He's hard and urgent, and his powerful energy surrounds me. He only thrusts a few times before I feel myself clench around him.

He grips my ass, and I'm all the way there.

"Fastest orgasm...on...record," I pant out as I finish coming.

"Damn, Winter." His head drops to my shoulder. "I'm right behind you, babe."

I lock my ankles together as he comes, and as soon as he raises his head to meet my gaze, I say, "We're not going to sleep tonight, are we?"

He kisses me for a long time, and then he murmurs into my lips, "No fucking chance."

We may not get any sleep, but Hunter and I definitely make up for lost time. And every second of missed sleep is worth it.

He's worth it.

I love him. All those years apart, and we're both finally ready for the real thing.

Letting go of old dreams for new ones has never felt so good.

EPILOGUE

Hunter

I glance up at the clock. Less than a minute left.

We're running out of damn time.

I hustle my ass down the boards and slam into Declan Wild as he keeps the puck and maneuvers across the ice. Wild's a stickhandling master, and he's been successfully wasting time for over a minute already. No one from our team has been able to take the puck away from him.

The Montana Wild Kings are kicking our ass tonight. We won our first playoff series for our franchise in four games and then made it through the next one in six games before meeting the Wild Kings in the finals. We've taken them to seven games, but they're up three to one in this seventh and final game of the series that will determine the league champion.

Declan continues to skate around the ice like he's not being chased by six angry men. We cleared the goalie already, so it's all hands on deck to try to bring down Goliath.

But it won't be happening today.

The buzzer sounds, and the Wild Kings start celebrating on their home ice. Liam and I congratulate Jared and Max before he and I skate over to our bench and exit the ice for the last time this season.

I'm happy two of my brothers are champions.

But to get all the way to the end like that and then lose...

Stings like hell.

Then I glance up into the stands and see Winter clapping and looking right at me, and I realize how damn lucky I am.

I hold up my stick and point it at her.

In truth, I have very little to complain about.

This has been a crazy-good year.

I win my first league MVP. And I know New Orleans will get their own championship trophy soon. I'm going to be sure we bring a championship to my home city. I won't let that story end any other way.

And even more importantly, I have the love of my life by my side.

Winter stayed in New York for a month like she planned, and I flew there for opening night of Summerset Nights. Peyton and Ashley joined me along with Winter's parents.

Winter was phenomenal in her role. I know how hard she worked to get back to this level. To get over what that asshole did to her and stand on a stage again. But she told me she had no second thoughts about leaving when the show's run was over.

And so, when she was ready, I helped Winter pack up, and we came home to the bayou. She moved in with me. Some people may think we're moving too fast, but for Winter and me, it feels like it took a decade to finally end up where we belong—together.

She reached out to Les Anderson, and they were on the same page. Seems he'd been going around the city, trying to find a home for her musical. And he got one at a cool theater right off the French Quarter.

Winter asked Les if he would direct it, and he agreed but only if Winter played the lead. She said yes, and the two of them went about casting the rest of the characters.

Now, tonight is opening night, and I have a special surprise planned for afterward.

Jared and Max were able to fly in for Winter's performance, and I sit next to them and Liam, along with Murph, Ashley, Peyton and Scott, and Oliver and Blaire. Winter's parents are directly in front of us. Her mama's so thrilled; as she keeps telling me, if she'd known she could have the best of both, she would have urged her only child to stay in New Orleans years ago.

Winter nails her performance. She bows for the standing ovation at the end of the night, and when I catch her eye, she gives me a little wave.

I wink, hoping she knows how proud I am of her.

She was willing to change plans and follow her heart. To learn how to be kind to herself and still follow her ambitions.

I also know what it took for me to open up my heart again after losing both my parents. And the only woman I could ever love is standing on that stage before me.

After the show, I go backstage with a bouquet of roses for her.

We're in her dressing room, and Winter thanks me as she buries her face in the roses to sniff them.

"Ouch!" She brings her head up and stares into the roses.

I hide my smile. "Everything okay?"

"Yes, it's just that I banged my nose on someth—" She pulls out a shiny piece of jewelry. "Hunter? What is this?"

I take the ring out of her hand and drop down on one knee. "It's exactly what it looks like."

She puts her hands over her mouth.

"Winter Princess Allen, I love you. I will always love and respect and cherish you. Will you marry me?"

I didn't think I'd be nervous. I'm used to being in the spotlight and needing to deliver in the clutch. And yet, here I am with shaking hands, hoping the woman I love will say yes.

"Yes." She drops to her knees, and I slip the ring on her finger.

I take her chin in my hand and kiss her to seal the deal.

We're still kissing when there's a loud bang on her dressing room door.

"Can we come in?" Ashley's voice says.

Winter laughs. "Sure."

Ashley and Peyton barge through the door with Murph and my three nosy brothers in tow.

"Well?" Jared stares at us. "I got his plan out of him, Win. So you may as well tell us first—are y'all getting hitched?"

"We are," she says.

He scoops her up in his arms for a hug, and then he, Liam, Max, and Murph pound my back.

Ashley has some gold squares in her hand, and she takes her water bottle and starts soaking a paper towel from the stash on Winter's dressing table.

"What the hell are you doing?" I ask Ashley.

"Giving us all some temporary tats, a perk of my job. To celebrate your engagement in style." She presses a square onto my upper arm and holds a wet paper towel over it.

When she peels off the backing, I stare down at a glittery gold *NOLA Groom* design on my arm.

"*NOLA Groom?*" Jared breaks into laughter. "That's pretty funny."

Ashley grabs his arm and presses a square and then a wet paper towel onto him next. When she peels off the backing—

"*For Better or Worse?*" He squints at the design tattooed on his arm. "Is that a gold dick pic below the words?"

Ashley smirks at him. "It's not an actual picture. It's a design to match the slogan. That's what you get for making fun of my work accessories."

"I wasn't making fun!" he protests as he tries to wipe off the tattoo.

To no avail. I try, too, but those suckers hold.

Ashley works her way around our circle, and before long, all of us but Max, who claimed some BS allergy to adhesives, are wearing *NOLA Squad* tattoos on our arms. Winter's also sporting a *NOLA Bride* and a *Much Hap-penis* tattoo that has another—as Jared said—"gold dick pic."

"Are you satisfied?" Peyton asks Ashley. "I think you've accessorized the hell out of all of us."

"Very," Ashley says as she hugs Winter. "I want to remember my best girl's engagement."

Not to be outdone, Murph and Jared insist on throwing us an impromptu engagement party.

"At my house," Murph says. "I've got my hot tub now."

I guess that makes it a win-win.

Winter takes my hand, and we head out of the dressing room. Jared's always looking for any excuse to party, and I can hear him calling people as we walk to the parking lot.

As soon as we arrive at Murph's house, I pull Winter onto my lap, and we hang out by the pool area in the backyard.

The hot tub is filled with women in bikinis, and I don't think any of us actually know who they are.

I watch as two of the women approach Max. He barely gives them the time of day as he sidesteps their attempts to touch him and heads over to me. He's nearly made it to us when a loud scream makes us all turn toward the pool.

A woman is hanging off the high diving board—her hands are gripping the board, but instead of dropping fully into the water, she's screaming and laughing.

Something makes me glance back at Max.

His jaw tightens, but what's impossible to miss is the obvious panic in his eyes.

He freezes in place, his gaze focused on the woman like she needs saving.

I tell Winter I'll be right back, and she stands so I can get up.

"What's up?" I ask Max when I reach him.

His face is white as he points at the dangling woman.

"She's okay," I assure him.

As if on cue, the woman finally lets go of the board and drops into the water. She bobs right back up and swims to the side and climbs out.

"See?" I tilt my head in her direction. "She's fine."

Max lets out a deep exhale. The blood slowly returns to his face, and he blinks like he barely realized what just happened.

This is something Liam, Jared, and I have all seen Max go through before. We never know why or when he'll check out. Liam assumes it's something to do with Dad's murder, and he convinced Max to talk to a therapist. I'm not sure it's helped.

"Hey." I grab his shoulder. "Let's go sit down."

He follows me over to where Winter and Peyton are sitting on chaise lounges.

Winter stands so I can return to our shared seating, and then she slips back onto my lap as Max drops down into the empty chair next to us.

As Winter returns to her conversation with Peyton on our other side, I lean in closer to Max.

"You okay?" I say to him in a low voice. "You look a little spooked."

Understatement, but I don't want to push him because he'll just shut down more.

"Fine." He shakes his head as if to clear some memory. "I think I'm going to get something to drink. Be right back."

I let him go. Because I know my brother. He's not going to talk to me right now.

Ashley wanders over to join us, and I smile when she complains about all the random women.

"My brother's influence," I say. "Jared won't settle down."

"He's not even talking to any of them, though," Winter points out.

That's true, actually.

"Why the hell did Jared invite them then?" Ashley says curtly. "They're puck bunnies. It's pretty obvious they only want one thing."

Jared, beer in hand, squeezes into the chaise lounge next to Ashley.

"Hey, y'all."

Ashley rolls her eyes at him. "Seriously, why invite all these strangers over if you're not even going to hang out with them?"

Jared glances over at the hot tub. "They bothering you?"

Ashley blushes. "No. Yes. I don't know!"

She looks at Peyton, who stands up and the two of them head for the house.

I shake my head at my brother. "Jared, what are you doing?"

He just grins. "I didn't invite them for me. I invited them for Liam."

"Liam?" Winter looks around. "Where is he? Besides being married, that is."

"He's hiding out inside. He and Cathy are on the outs," Jared says. "He's having a rough go of it."

Winter turns to me. "You didn't mention that. I would have baked him something."

I kiss her neck. "You still can. I didn't know if he wanted his situation known yet. It's still pretty raw."

Jared and I exchange worried glances.

"I'm going to go check on him," Jared says. "And maybe I'll try to make up with Ashley."

"Whatever happened between you two?" I ask him.

He just flips me off and keeps walking. "None of your business, Hunt," he calls over his shoulder.

Winter turns to me. "I can't believe Ashley never spilled to me. She's usually an open book."

I shrug. "Maybe we'll find out someday. In the meanwhile, do you want to get out of here?"

Winter smiles. "You have some post-engagement party plans for us?"

Absolutely.

I want to take my fiancée in my arms and tell her how much I love her.

How much I've always loved her.

"I vote for going straight to the bedroom," she whispers to me.

I kiss her as we stand up. "We're on the same page, Princess," I say in her ear.

Winter and I spent so many years on different pages while we chased our dreams. And I'm a lucky guy to have a second chance to make up for what we missed.

I count my blessings that we were given the opportunity to reconnect. I never forgot the blue-eyed girl who helped me wash away the stain of loss, but I also never thought I'd be able to welcome her back into my life. Then, fate stepped in and put Winter right at my front door. And, despite my guarded heart, I let her in.

And like it's always been with Winter, she gave me far more than I expected anyone could. She always has.

To give my heart to Winter, and to share a future together forever, is the best—and easiest—decision I ever made.

ANOTHER EPILOGUE

Emerson

I race through the crowded hockey arena, my camera slung over my shoulder as I follow the moving puck with my gaze. As the Montana Wild Kings take control of the puck and cross the blue line, I freeze in the aisle about ten rows from the ice.

"Hey! Take a seat!" someone yells from behind me.

Without taking my eyes off the game, I crouch down on the aisle steps and watch as Montana's first-line left-winger and the opposing defenseman bang up against the boards. I'm so close I can hear the players cursing each other out as they fight for the puck. And then—

Crash!

The boards shake as a third player barrels into the fray. He pokes at the puck with his stick, effortlessly dislodging it from the Florida defender and taking off down the ice.

"There he is!" the woman says from the seat next to where I'm standing.

I inhale a sharp breath. Yes, there he is.

Max Storm.

I haven't seen him in over a decade, and my hands are shaking so much I clench them into fists.

He's no longer the boy I crushed on as a teenager. He's a man now. One thing hasn't changed, though—I'm still the girl on the sidelines cheering him on while he shines so bright the whole arena can't take their eyes off of him.

"The rumor is Storm won't let any woman touch him," my nosy neighbor shout whispers.

"He must not date then," her friend says.

"I went on a date with him," a third female says confidently.

I unclench my fists and dig my nails into my jeans, using every ounce of willpower not to turn and look over at them.

"Did he let you touch him?" the first woman asks.

Long pause.

I'm dying.

"No," she finally says in a sullen tone. "All he wanted to do was take me as his date to a required charity event. He wouldn't even let me put out afterward. I mean, who does that? Look at me!"

Okay, now I sneak a peek.

Yeah, she's pretty. Blonde, tanned, despite it being winter. And she's confident. She knows she's attractive, and she wears that knowledge all over her fake-bronzed face.

I turn back to the ice.

Max may not let anyone touch him now, but he wasn't always that way.

He was my first kiss.

And my first heartbreak.

But that was years ago.

Long before he became a hockey star.

We didn't keep in contact. He has no idea I'm in Montana.

And I don't know if he'd even remember me at all.

That's the last thought I have before Max flicks his stick and the puck bounces off the defender. It heads straight for our section.

I feel cold, hard heaviness hit me square on the forehead.

And then, the world goes dark.

***

Max

Fuck.

I've played hockey for most of my life.

I've never once hit someone in the stands.

It would have been a goal if the damn lineman hadn't deflected the puck. Instead, my shot took somebody out. I stare up at the section where my errant puck went. Between the EMTs and the crowd, I can't see what the hell's going on.

As the refs call a timeout, I rush off the ice and over to the bench.

"Storm, don't go up there!" Coach Florio warns me. "Let the medical staff handle it."

Fuck that. I toss off my helmet and throw on my skate guards.

"I need to make sure they're all right," I say. "I'll come back in five." I turn and head up the stairs.

The person is hunched over in the aisle. Her long blond hair is covering her face, and I can't tell if she's conscious or not.

I step out of the way as our team doctor hurries ahead and bends down in front of her. After a few minutes of checking in with her, he signals to the two EMTs who are standing with a stretcher.

They carefully lift the woman and place her onto it.

I lean over the stretcher and peer into her face.

With all that blond hair, I can't see much of anything, but as I stare at her, a tightness hits my chest at the same time that warmth fills my body. I can't explain it.

I brush a chunk of her hair off her cheek. "Hey," I say softly. "Are you all right?"

Her eyes flutter open, and she stares up at me.

Gray-blue eyes fix on me in a way no one's have since...

My hand freezes on her hair, and I'm brought back to years ago. "Emmy?"

***

Thank you for reading HUNTER!

Continue reading the Storm Brothers with Book 2, **Max**.

Tap here for Max and Emerson's hot and steamy second chance story!

MAX

Get ready for Hunter's brother, Max! Max and Emerson's second chance story is hot and sweet. **Click Here**!

Take a peek at MAX:

Max Storm was my first kiss. My first crush.
And my first heartbreak.
Then, he became a hockey star.
Over a decade later...
I go to a game. And he accidentally hits me with a puck.
He's there when I regain consciousness.
His chocolate eyes lock onto mine, and I'm a goner.
He says he'll help me with the one first he couldn't give me all those years ago.
I just hope I'll be able to walk away after.
Because time spent with Max Storm is always fleeting...

TO READ *MAX,* **CLICK HERE!**

DECLAN

My one night stand is now my husband ... A MARRIAGE OF CONVENIENCE ROMANCE.

Mia

I don't do professional athletes. And I certainly don't do one-night stands.

But after my father tells me to marry before he'll let me take over his PR firm, which has been my one and only dream since I was a kid, I decide I need a night out.

And when a hot hockey player picks me out at the saloon in the heart of Montana, I decide I want to play.

He takes me to his home on a gorgeous ranch. We steam up the sheets all night long.

And in the morning, I leave him a thank you note and slip out while he's sleeping.

I'm sure I'll never see him again.

Until the next day, when my uncle introduces him as my future husband.

Declan

Before I retire from playing professionally, I'm lining up my next shot—an ownership stake in the Montana Wild Kings hockey team. But the team's got a PR problem, and they'll never approve a bachelor.

I'm not in a relationship. I'm not even dating.

And I can't remember the last time I was interested in someone. Until I go to the bar after the game to blow off some steam and figure out my next move.

That's when I meet her. Mia. The first woman I can remember who doesn't know I'm a big time hockey player.

After we spend an incredible night together, she bails.

I figure that's it.

Until my agent calls me into his office. The only other person in the room? Mia.

My future wife.

We vow to keep our arrangement strictly professional so we both get what we want. But the more we face off, the more I want to score...

Get the book here!

ACKNOWLEDGMENTS

Thank you to—
    To J. Hunter for your fabulous covers and artistry.
    To Dawn for always being flexible with my crazy schedule and of course for your gift of editing.
    To Mr. B for being my go-to on everything sports-related.
    To my mom for taking me to skating lessons.
    To my husband for NOLA.
    To my children for letting mama write.
    To M and M for the cuddles.
    And to my readers for going on this journey with me.

ALSO BY MELISSA BELLE

Boston Boys

BOSTON BILLIONAIRE

BOSTON LOVE

BOSTON ESCAPE

BOSTON ROOMIE

BOSTON BAD BOY

BOSTON PLAYER

Wild Men

COLTON

DYLAN

AYDEN

JENSON

BRAYDEN

CAMERON

DECLAN

MICHAEL

LUKE

Wild Men Texas

WHISKEY GIRL

WARRIOR GIRL

WILD GIRL

Storm Brothers

HUNTER

JARED

MAX

LIAM

Bonus Wild Men Stories

WILD MAN (Colton and Sky prequel novella)

WILD VALENTINE (Ayden and Bella short story)

Sign up for Melissa's Newsletter to get a free story and to receive alerts
and updates on upcoming book releases.

BONUS FREE STORY!

Ayden and Bella Wild have everything they want...except one thing. Pick up **WILD VALENTINE** as a free bonus short story (complete with an HEA) **HERE**!

ABOUT THE AUTHOR

A USA Today Bestselling author, Melissa Belle is known for her contemporary romance style that's sweet, sexy, and smart. She writes hot, steamy romance with complex heroes and heroines. She spent years in the field of psychology before writing her first novel riding the train around Europe with her husband. Melissa likes cupcakes, road trips, and songwriting.

To receive an email when Melissa releases a new book, sign up for her VIP List!

www.melissabellebooks.com

Cover Art: J. Hunter Designs
Proofreading: Dawn Yacovetta

www.ingramcontent.com/pod-product-compliance
Lightning Source LLC
Chambersburg PA
CBHW071331250626
47159CB00004B/1556